WOULD IT BE OKAY TO LOVE YOU?

Year Three

AMY TASUKADA

ACKNOWLEDGMENTS

THANK YOU TO MY family. Without your support, I wouldn't be able to have the time to follow my dream and write. The Dallas Area Romance Author group whose brainstorming session helped with many of the ideas for Aoi and Sato. Legne Hardt, your plotting help is magical and breaks through all of my blocks. Nell Iris and Addison Albright, thank you for always being my go-to writing buddies and double-checking that I didn't kill anyone in the romance books and piss people off. Haha. A special thanks goes out to Maija. Thank you for helping Aoi and Sato be the best goldfish pet parents they can be. Also to all my readers: thank you for helping Aoi and Sato come to life all these years.

OCTOBER

AOI PULLED AT THE ends of his dyed blond hair. He needed a haircut. Another thing they could judge him for.

The last time he'd prepared so much was for his high school entrance exam, and that was more than a decade ago. He shuffled through to the next index card.

He sank deeper into his seat as the train rolled to a stop. Not his stop. He still had time to look over his speech in the vain hope he'd look prepared.

"Relax." Sato pushed up his dark-framed glasses, making them more askew. He turned into the cutest salaryman when it happened. "You'll be fine."

The height difference between Aoi and his boyfriend was apparent even sitting. Aoi had never met anyone shorter than himself except for maybe a passing elementary student, and he'd never met anyone taller than Sato. They probably looked funny sitting side by side. A perfect example of opposites, but Sato completed Aoi in every way. Aoi hoped he could do the same for him.

Aoi shook his head and thumbed through the next card. "I hope it's good enough."

"It will be. You've been practicing for two weeks."

"I still can't believe your mom asked me."

"Well, her son is dating the biggest gay icon in Japan. Of course everyone in the Association of LGBT Family and Friends meeting would see if she could get you to talk."

Sato kept his voice low to not disturb anyone else on the train, but Aoi's face grew hot. Had he known coming out on a small television show would result in the story being picked up by national news, he doubted he would've had the courage to come out as gay. He should've known better. His voice acting made him a D-list celebrity, but once the gossip machine got wind of the story, it'd blown the whole thing out of proportion.

"I'm not such a big deal," Aoi said.

"I think you are."

He placed his hand on the small space between them on the bench, and Sato did the same, their pinkies touching while the rest of them couldn't.

Aoi's racing heart slowed. Even straight couples got odd looks for public displays of affection, so they didn't want to risk it.

"I'll fold the cards into knives and stab out my eyeballs if I look at these anymore." Aoi shoved the cards into his pants pocket.

"You speak for a living, so it will come naturally once you're there."

"That's me alone in a recording studio, not speaking to a bunch of people with them staring at my face. Even with live reads, I read off the script and have other actors to bounce off of. Here it's my life story of neglect."

"I'll sit right up front, so focus on me."

Aoi pressed his lips together. "That might help."

"Anything you need, I'll be there."

They were still five stops away, and Aoi's leg jiggled more with every stop. He cleared his throat, hoping that would open his airway, but it didn't.

"Tell me something," Aoi said.

"I love you."

"I already know that. Something to distract me."

Sato laughed. "It's cute seeing you get flustered before speaking for once."

"Cute?" Aoi cocked an eyebrow.

"Because I know you'll be awesome."

"You're not helping."

Sato chuckled. "Okay, let's see. The manga writer for *Wild Skies* finally started again. The newest chapter is coming out next month."

"That's that Gundam one you were telling me about. They, like, battle aliens, right?"

"They're called the Freak. It's so good. They battle in space to protect the few remaining humans stuck on different spaceships as they travel to find a new home world…"

Aoi nodded along as Sato continued to talk about the fun twists and turns to the series. Sato had been caught up rereading the series since the artist had announced his hiatus was over. Aoi had heard about some of them before, but it proved to be a good distraction. Sato was so excited about it, Aoi suspected it would be Sato's new favorite, but that changed every few months.

"There've been some more rumors of an anime series coming, but those have been on and off for years." Sato shrugged. "It might be fun, but I'm not getting my hopes up."

"Do the robots kiss?"

"Not yet."

"Hmm… the newest release they will. The artist will go in a bold, new direction."

"The old fans might not enjoy the change."

Aoi leaned back. "But so many new ones will enjoy the new boys' love angle. It'll make up for it."

The playful banter they'd always shared and the normalcy of it all slowed Aoi's thumping heart. Sato obsessed over almost every Gundam series, but Aoi read the newest gay romance manga with the same vigor. Aoi cracked a smile. He got to say it was for voice acting research though, while the robots had nothing to do with Sato's accounting job other than doing the numbers for their budgets.

The train came to their stop, and Aoi and Sato got out. They strolled to the building where the meeting would take place.

"I'm so glad you were able to come," Emi, Sato's mother, said.

Her smile glowed like Sato's and helped to ease some of the last few nerves buzzing within Aoi. When they'd first met, there were no smiles. It was Aoi's parents all over again, but slowly Emi had come around. Sato and Aoi's monthly visits to his family were filled with joy, and at least once a week Emi would email Aoi a recipe she thought he'd enjoy.

She escorted them to the meeting room and introduced them to the board. Everyone shared Emi's smile.

More and more people flooded the small room. Soon enough, the twenty or so chairs were filled, even after the director took some extra chairs out of the closet. But a few minutes after that, it became standing room only.

Aoi gulped. "I thought you said it was a small membership."

"Usually only a dozen people attend the meetings," Emi said.

Sato squeezed his shoulder. "They must've heard you were speaking."

"Is it time to get started?" Aoi's foot tapped out the beat of his rising temperature. "Maybe they'll stop entering if I'm already talking."

Sato gave Aoi a knowing look, but Aoi wasn't having any guilt. Emi found the president, and they started the meeting. Aoi sat beside Sato in the front row with the reserved seating. Sato reached across Aoi's lap and squeezed his hand. Even if Sato hadn't said anything, Aoi could hear his reassuring words in his smile.

Aoi's throat tickled like when he'd screamed too much at a rock concert. He pulled the note cards out of his pocket and flipped through each one, the little doodle of himself saying "you can do it" in the corners. He'd read lines from a script hundreds of times, and he could pretend his speech was another fictionalized piece—one that mirrored his life exactly. Aoi bit the inside of his cheek. No anime would ever tackle the real-life hardship of being shoved out the house by homophobic parents. No one would want to watch something so depressing.

"So, let me introduce the talented Aoi Hirayama," Emi cheered.

Aoi approached the microphone, and the audience clapped. It was taller than him, so in a quick second he shortened it and stared out at everyone. So many people in business suits, like they'd taken off work to hear him speak. Sure, Sato had too, but he was different. Aoi had figured he'd be speaking to a few housewives and a half-dozen retirees, not people who reminded him so much of his parents.

Sato's and Emi's smiles couldn't be bigger, so Aoi tried to focus on them.

"Thanks, everyone." Aoi rubbed a sweaty palm on his jeans and cleared his throat.

He clutched the cards. Maybe he should've typed them up like a script, and then he could've doodled bigger reassuring characters on the side. How could he get worried if his sketched goldfish was telling him he was the best?

"This is a little different than the studios I record in."

The audience chuckled.

That was good. His first joke landed. People liked to laugh. He pulled the cards close to his face, but knew that wasn't right. He'd talked to a group of people before, and he knew to lower the cards so they could see his face. To project his voice. But it was everything he couldn't do. He couldn't look at their faces, and staring in one direction would look odd.

Someone coughed, and Aoi flipped to the next card, but his sweaty hand made it stick.

"I grew up in a normal household like everyone else," Aoi said from memory. "My parents wanted the best out of me. I worked in their restaurant during the weekend from since I could remember."

The words clung to his throat as if they had hooks, ripping his vocal cords on the way out. They were a secret not meant to be told in polite society. No one really wanted to hear them, and they didn't want to be heard.

Aoi balled his hand into a fist. The fact no one wanted to hear them was the reason they needed to be told. Any mild discomfort was nothing compared to the years of pain he'd faced. Aoi slipped the cards into his pocket and grabbed the microphone out of the stand. It screeched. He pulled it away.

"Look," Aoi said. "Maybe you were expecting a nice biography of how my hard work turned me into a successful voice actor, but I was lucky. Most people who started out like me are lucky if they scrape by. Many end up dead."

More coughing and a few stern looks, but Sato's smile warmed Aoi's throbbing heart and eased the pain in his throat.

"When I was a teen, my parents found out I was gay and kicked me out. There was no question. There was no pretending it didn't exist. I was dead to them. In an instant, I was homeless. How could I even think of finishing school or going to college when I didn't have enough money to eat? I scraped by, sleeping in the back of the convenience store I was lucky enough to get hired at, since I didn't have an address. When that didn't work, I would have one-night stands to get a bed for the night. It was shitty."

Aoi rubbed his throat. Maybe "shitty" wasn't the right word for a public meeting, but it got the point across. More concerned faces stared back at him. Good. They were understanding.

"So, remember not everyone is like the people who join the Association of LGBT Family and Friends. A lot of people aren't even like Mrs. Emi, who might've not understood at first but loved her son enough to learn and accept. More than accept. If you take away anything from this short speech, please let it be that you can become the family of those that have none. Give or volunteer at shelters if you can." Aoi placed his hand over his heart. "I'm gonna do my best to make sure people don't think the love I feel in my heart is some kind of hobby. My sexuality is not the odd nail that needs to be hammered down."

Even as Aoi's throat grew raw with emotion, everyone applauded. Aoi thanked everyone and walked back to his seat.

"I knew you could do it," Sato said.

"Only because you were here with me." Aoi's voice sputtered out halfway and became nothing but a whisper.

Sato stood. "Let me get you some water. All that practicing must've worn out your voice."

Aoi nodded.

"Mrs. Emi." Aoi cleared his throat to strengthen his voice. "I wanted to say thanks for asking me. My agent's been calling me to do so many interviews, but this one is the most important one I've given."

She smiled. "No, thank you for helping me grow. I really think without you, I wouldn't have truly known my son."

Sato brought him water, and he nodded a thank-you. Aoi ran his finger along the rim of the cup and took a sip. It helped but only temporarily. The only other time his voice strained so much had been after a solid week of recording dialogue. It shouldn't have hurt so much after a few days of practicing a speech under twenty minutes.

Aoi put his palm on his throat and pressed against his Adam's apple as he drank a few more deep sips of the water.

"You okay?" Sato pushed up his glasses. "I can see if they have any tea."

"I'll be fine," Aoi said, but each word he spoke felt like double the effort.

Sato shook his head and turned to his mom. "We should probably get going. People will want to talk to Aoi, and he shouldn't strain his voice anymore."

She agreed, refilling Aoi's cup and letting them go on their way.

Aoi nursed the drink all the way to the train station. He glanced to Sato and smiled, but Sato's eyebrows drew together. How he'd ended up with the most caring Gundam otaku, Aoi never knew, but the look of concern stabbed his heart.

"You sure you'll be all right?"

Aoi grinned. "I think once we get home you'll know exactly the best medicine to serve me."

"Oh will I?"

"You can play doctor and get me to open my mouth and say ahh."

NOVEMBER

T HE BIG MIRRORS AND huge lightbulbs were so different from the black egg-crate-foam-lined closets of the recording studio. Aoi could've shown up to work in his pajamas and no one would've cared, but since he'd become one of the minor hosts for a TV variety show, he'd gotten someone to choose his clothes for him.

"You'd look so cute with lip gloss. Are you sure you don't want to try?" the makeup lady asked, her long bleached curls bouncing with her excitement.

Aoi tried to resist but ended up cracking a smile. "You ask that every time, and I always say no."

"I want to see if you'll change your mind." She fanned out a few different shades of pink and nude tubes in front of Aoi. "Please, this one would go great with your hair."

"Do you ask the other male hosts this?"

"All the time!" She lit up and then frowned. "They say no too."

"Maybe tomorrow."

"I'll hold you to it."

"I know you will."

She patted Aoi's nose with some powder. "Atsushi told me you two paired up for some recordings."

Aoi's stomached turned. "We worked professionally on a few projects."

"His voice is so dreamy. Yours is fine too, but his is so deep and sexy."

"That's why he plays the dominant role in the romances."

Aoi cleared his throat, and the makeup lady handed him the cup of tea he'd left on the counter. The warm liquid coated his throat, washing away the crud clogging around his vocal cords. It always felt like he needed to take one more gulp to get it all clean, but no matter how much he drank, the feeling returned.

Atsushi poked his head into the room. "There you are."

"How nice to see you again." Aoi's tone dropped.

Atsushi strolled in and put his hands on Aoi's shoulders. Aoi's muscles tensed as he stared straight ahead. Atsushi's long dark hair contrasted against Aoi's blond, and he loomed over him in the mirror.

"You did an awesome job with his hair," Atsushi said. "Love the cool little spikes on the sides."

"Are we done?" Aoi asked.

The makeup lady patted Aoi's forehead. "Unless you want to try the lip gloss."

Atsushi laughed. "She asked me that one too."

"Did you change your mind, Atsushi?"

He grinned. "You know what? Why not? You can give it to me."

She bounced and held up a few tubes from light nude to a dark red. Atsushi leaned forward, his breath tickling Aoi's ear. He couldn't be more purposely in the way.

"What color do you want?" she asked.

"Surprise me." Atsushi opened his mouth, his hand still clutching Aoi's shoulder.

She cleared her throat as Aoi rolled his eyes. The way Atsushi abused his looks to make people uncomfortable was disgusting. She finished, and Atsushi pouted his glossy pale pink lips.

"What do you think, Aoi?" Atsushi's face drew so close they could be kissing.

Aoi backed away. "It's wonderful."

The makeup woman asked Atsushi something, and Aoi took the opportunity to slip out of the chair.

Aoi fled the room, taking his tea and hiding next to the curtain separating the backstage from the live audience. He managed to finish his tea in peace, but then Atsushi slinked over. Aoi grimaced, then reminded himself not to make a big scene about it before they were due onstage. Atsushi loved bugging him and getting off on all the attention.

"You still trying to hide from me after everything I did for you?" Atsushi said.

Aoi crossed his arms. "The only thing you've done for me was make me late for my Christmas date."

"And give you the best advice of your career. Does it mean nothing to you? I deserve a reward for making you a household name."

"You can kiss my ass if you think you'll get shit out of me."

Atsushi laughed, took a step closer, and looked down at Aoi. Atsushi played up his height. It might've worked, but Aoi's boyfriend was a giant. Still, Aoi couldn't help but look away.

"No wonder you play submissive so well. You act like one. I was thinking we could start dating. Then it can be a win-win situation."

"I'm already dating someone."

"Then we can fake it. People do it all the time."

Aoi's fingers flexed, craving to punch Atsushi's face for the suggestion. They had to give a live interview in a few minutes, and getting into a fight with the guest star would cost Aoi his job. Aoi shoved his hands into his pockets.

"It will be better for both of our careers," Atsushi said. "If you don't believe me, call up your agent. She'll love the idea."

"I said no."

"Fine, fine." He held up his hands. "It's sad since everyone loves it when we're together. You can't blame me for wishing you'd do something else with me again after getting those residual checks in the mail from our past project."

"It sounds like you're trying to leech off my popularity. You're lucky I didn't put a clause in my contract with this show that said you were banned from appearing."

"You made sure to include the one about the *no kissing games*. Are you sure you want to keep to it?"

Aoi brushed past Atsushi onto the stage, to the waiting live audience. They cheered when he appeared, and Aoi smiled. At least he could hide from Atsushi in the open. He chatted with the crowd for a bit, and then the other hosts joined. There were five hosts in total, though most of the talking was done by an older man and woman. Everyone else sat on the back sofa and were used for reaction shots, and then were dragged onto the main stage when a segment would be funny if they were included.

It was the easiest job Aoi had ever had, and sometimes the different experts they interviewed were fun. Yesterday they had a golf star who'd taught Aoi the perfect putt. Sometimes they had actors or other professionals. One time they had a baker, and everyone got to learn how to decorate a cupcake. Aoi had brought his creation home for Sato to enjoy.

The host introduced Atsushi and spoke to him about his upcoming project about a sport fishing anime. He played the lead in a cast of five beautiful boys who made every lady who watched dream about putting the characters together, while learning more about fishing than they had ever wanted to know.

"Are you good at fishing?" the main host asked Atsushi.

He laughed. "I did it a few times when I was a kid."

"Well, we got some fish here, so let's go see. Aoi, why don't you come too?"

It took a few minutes for the studio to get set up, but then several brightly colored toy robot fish roamed an enclosed area off the stage. Everyone was given a kid's fishing pole and attempted to catch them.

The audience cheered as Atsushi cast his line and landed a toy fish on his first go. Aoi's cast landed nowhere near any of the fish and almost hit one of the camera operators. It got a chuckle from everyone.

"What was the largest fish you caught?" the host asked.

"Maybe this big." Atsushi held out his hands a reasonable length apart.

"Said like a perfect fishing master."

Aoi laughed. "Does it get bigger each time you tell it?"

"What about you?"

"I only cooked the fish."

"What kind do you like to cook best?" Atsushi asked, casting off another line.

"I'm really good at mackerel. I usually put it on the grill and infuse it with herbs." Aoi swallowed to cleanse his dry throat. "It goes well with potatoes and mushrooms."

"Maybe you can cook it for me sometime."

Aoi's eyes narrowed. Atsushi couldn't be serious, trying to fake-flirt with him on stage. Of course he was. Atsushi wouldn't care about Aoi's blanket disapproval; he only cared about what to do to boost his approval with his fans so they'd buy more stuff.

Atsushi tilted his head to the side. "Come on. It sounds like the perfect date."

"That's right, you are bisexual," the male host said.

There was an audience gasp and whispers.

Atsushi stepped closer to Aoi. "What do you say? Is it a date?"

Aoi took a big step away from Atsushi, getting a laugh out of the audience. "I already have a boyfriend. We've been together for many years."

Atsushi shrugged. "Maybe next time, then."

At least the rest of the show went off without any more hints of dating. The other secondary hosts took over, letting Aoi stay behind for the reaction shots.

Once the show was over, the audience clapped and Aoi was handed his usual post-shoot cup of ginger tea. Atsushi stood behind him, using his full height to Aoi's disadvantage.

"I was wrong, about what I said before," Atsushi said.

"Is that your shitty way to apologize?"

Aoi took a step back out to avoid Atsushi's looming frame. Atsushi laughed, sending a shiver down Aoi's spine. Atsushi could be such a creep.

"How long has your voice been messed up?"

Aoi clutched the mug a little tighter. "I don't know what you're talking about."

"It's breathy when you talk. And not in the good way, if you know what I mean."

"I'm fine."

"Has a doctor checked it out yet?"

"Can you leave me alone?"

Aoi turned to leave, but Atsushi grabbed his arm. Aoi tensed. Who did Atsushi think he was? Aoi jerked his arm free. The tea in his cup splashed out and sloshed onto the floor.

"I want to act with you again," Atsushi said. "What I'm saying is from one professional to another here. Get your voice looked at soon, or you might regret waiting so long."

"Whatever."

"Maybe no one else can hear it, but I can. You've chosen to do these variety TV shows not because you would be seen by everyone in Japan on a daily basis but because your voice couldn't handle a voice actor's recording schedule."

Aoi bit the inside of his cheek, but the pain was felt throughout his body. Atsushi had figured him out better than even Sato could. His voice couldn't sustain more than a five-minute conversation, let alone eight hours of recording. Aoi curled his lip, and Atsushi patted him on the shoulder.

"Hope you listen to my advice again," he said then walked off.

Aoi closed his eyes and rubbed them. He was screwed. If Atsushi could hear the difference, then any director would. What would Aoi do if he couldn't voice-act anymore?

DECEMBER

S ATO STROLLED DOWN THE street on the way to the café. When he had agreed to the double date with Jiro and Chie, he'd assumed Aoi would have the days leading up to New Year's off. Sadly, he was wrong. When Aoi had said the variety TV show he worked on recorded every weekday, he really meant *every* day, national holidays included. Sato hadn't said anything negative about it, even if he'd wanted to spend his first day of his vacation snuggling in bed, but having to give Aoi up for half a day wasn't too bad.

Aoi had enjoyed his work for the variety show, and they'd fallen into a good rhythm over the past month. Aoi would have dinner ready when Sato got home, and then they'd watch a recording of the show together. Aoi would tell him little behind-the-scenes stories between kisses.

Sato sighed, daydreaming about Aoi's luscious lips and the way his collarbones were perfect for licking. His cock stirred. Probably shouldn't think too much about it in public. Sato texted Jiro that he'd arrived and entered the café.

It was cute. A yellow building with a cutout bee next to the name. A junky-looking antique store stood across the street, but it was easily ignored. A large decal of a thick square of honey bread dominated the wall with the name of the café, Sweet Honey, written in dripping font. The other walls were a soft lavender and yellow color.

Sato's stomach rumbled. With the amount of people crowded inside, everything had to be good.

"We're back here." Jiro waved to Sato.

Sato followed Jiro past the display case of tasty treats and entered a small honey-colored back room. The door shut behind them, muffling the noise of the outside. A small table stood in the center with four chairs stuffed around it. A few bite-sized pieces of cake were on the table.

Chie look up from a large photo album of cakes when they entered the room.

"Sato, you remember Chie," Jiro said.

She pushed her long black hair over her shoulder. "Thank you so much for coming."

"Anytime. It's too bad Aoi couldn't make it," Sato said.

"But you're not dating your sister, so it worked out fine. I'm glad, since Michiko was a little… different."

"That's for sure. Let me grab something to eat, and I'll join you." Sato chuckled. He was never going to live down the day he faked a date before coming out.

When Sato had told Jiro Aoi couldn't make it to the double date, Sato had assumed it would be canceled, but Jiro had insisted that Chie didn't mind. Jiro was his best friend, so

Sato went with it. It allowed him to indulge his sweet tooth, since Aoi was more health conscious.

Sato lingered by the display case. Each artistic-looking dessert looked better than the next after the next before getting in line. Even then he debated between the chocolate cake or the strawberry mousse cake. He and Aoi had chocolate cake for Christmas, but the one at the cafe had cherries mixed in. Yet the strawberry one always felt more like New Year's.

"Hey, sexy," Aoi said.

Sato turned and smiled. "You made it."

"We got done early."

Sato raised an eyebrow. Usually Aoi would be gone a few more hours. He hadn't been gone long enough to make it through a whole show.

"Am I too late for cake?" Aoi asked.

"No. Jiro and Chie snagged a room to themselves so it can feel like a proper double date."

"Lucky us." Aoi glanced at the cakes. "If I get the strawberry, will you get the chocolate?"

"You read my mind."

The line moved up, and Aoi unwrapped the blue scarf from around his neck.

"Is Chie really as bad as Michiko made her out to be?" Aoi asked.

Sato rubbed his neck. "Jiro has been dating her forever, so she has to be okay."

"Michiko said I should pretend to trip and throw my drink on her."

"You need to stop talking to my sister when no one is around." Sato shook his head. "I swear sometimes she thinks you're a combination of all the manga characters you've acted."

"She has crossed the line a few times, but she means well… I think."

Sato laughed. "Maybe in her own twisted world where people can't die of embarrassment."

They reached the front of the line and ordered their cakes. Aoi added a ginger tea to the order.

"You've been enjoying that ginger tea lately," Sato said. They moved to the side of the register while their drinks were being made.

"My throat's a little scratchy today."

"It's been like that for a while now, hasn't it?"

Sato had lost count of the number of times he'd woken up to the sound of Aoi gargling salt water. There had even been a few days earlier in the month where he was so hoarse, he sounded like he had smoked a pack of cigarettes a day since he was seven. All the times Sato had asked about it, Aoi had brushed it off, but Sato could sense an underlying unease lingering underneath Aoi's reassurances. His voice had never acted up for as long as they'd dated. It was odd. Something had to be going on that Aoi hadn't been telling him.

Aoi shrugged. "It's the weather."

"I guess when we get older, different allergies affect us more."

"You're right there next to all the tree pollen. I'm surprised you don't get hay fever with how tall you are."

They grabbed their drinks and made their way back to Jiro and Chie. They exchanged greetings and sat down. Aoi snatched a forkful of Sato's chocolate cake while Sato did the same with Aoi's.

"How's the German chocolate?" Chie asked.

"I like it," Sato said. "But the strawberry is a bit fluffier."

Aoi nodded. "They're both good, but it depends on what kind of mood you're in."

Chie tapped her fork against her lips and turned to Jiro. "Do you want something more light or dense?"

"It's like Aoi said, what mood do you want? Maybe what we had before? You know, it reminds me of this one time when I was younger. My parents threw me a surprise party, and it was so wonderful. They had my favorite food, mac 'n cheese, and I ate so much of it, but then I didn't realize we had a cake too. I was really young—it's funny how when you're younger you do the whole 'if you don't see it, then it doesn't exist' thing. So since the cake…"

Jiro went on, like he always did, but Chie listened attentively. There was something romantic about it since most of the time Sato tuned out most of Jiro's long-winded stories.

"I never had a big party for my birthday," Chie said once Jiro came to a pause. "You know, I was thinking, Sato, it's a bit ironic that you were pretending to date Michiko, who was a totally gross fujoshi, and now here you are dating a boys' love voice actor. It must be hard for you to deal with her, right?"

Aoi tapped his fork on the plate. "I'm actually really glad there are people like Michiko. They help get me work." Aoi pushed his plate with the last pieces of strawberry cake to Sato, who shook his head.

"But don't you think you're being fetishized by them?"

Aoi stabbed the last piece of cake. "Isn't the whole romance genre fetishizing all relationships?"

"Yeah, but most BL is written by women. That's wrong."

"But don't they write in a man's point of view in straight romances too? Is it wrong then?"

"I mean—"

"I'm glad about every BL title that's published. The more of them out there, the better." Aoi looked toward Sato. "I know you read BL stuff when you were young. Didn't you enjoy it?"

Sato nodded. "It was nice to see more people like me."

"I read more magazines, but I love being able to play characters like me. If those women hadn't written it, then I couldn't act in their dramas. I might have an issue with some of the rapey ones, but those are the tropes, and even straight fiction has some tropes that make people cringe."

Sato had seen people like her online thinking they knew the feelings of all the gay community because they knew one person. She might've meant well, but it wasn't really about one person but society as a whole. One more book was one more out there for someone to identify with, to change their mind.

"Not every series is going to please everyone," Sato said, "but the more of it there is, the more normalized my relationship with Aoi will be to others."

"Yeah, Chie," Jiro said. "Everyone has their own thing. I think if anyone, Aoi would be the expert on this issue."

Chie gnawed on her bottom lip then passed the plate of two light-colored cake bites to Jiro. "Do you like the chocolate or honey more?"

"I don't know." Jiro tapped his lip. "The chocolate was nice, but the honey reminded me of this time we went on vacation to Okinawa…"

Jiro went on, and Chie passed the plate in front of Sato and Aoi.

"Which of these two do you like more?" She turned her attention back to Jiro.

Aoi looked at Sato curiously, but Sato shrugged. Jiro smiled, and they cut the small cakes in half with their forks and ate.

"Chocolate," they both said in unison.

Chie smiled. "Chocolate cake for the wedding it is."

Sato pushed up his glasses. "Wedding?"

"You were supposed to tell him already."

Jiro gave a nervous laugh. "I kept on meaning to tell him, but then we changed topics and it was hard to get it back."

"Congratulations!" Aoi cheered. "When's the date?"

"August," Chie said, "and thanks for helping with the cake selection. I wanted the taste buds of a few people for the cake, and since I never got to meet you, Aoi, I figured it would be good to get both at the same time."

Jiro cleared his throat and sat up in his chair. "Also, Sato, you're my best friend—"

"You didn't even ask him that yet?"

"Weddings never came up in conversation." Jiro turned back to Sato. "I was hoping, if you don't mind, if you'll be my best man at the wedding. It would be an honor to have you there when Chie and I tie the knot."

Sato smiled. "I'd be happy to."

They chatted for a few more minutes, but with their drinks finished and Chie needing to hash out a few more cake design details with the baker, they parted ways.

Sato walked beside Aoi on the way to the train station. Aoi was quiet, which added a weight to Sato's chest. He knew something wasn't right.

"So are you going to tell me what really happened at the studio?" Sato asked.

Aoi pressed his lips together. "I don't really…"

"Was it something to do with why you're drinking tea so much lately?"

Aoi stared at the ground. Sato briefly put a hand on Aoi's shoulder, quick enough not to catch anyone's attention.

"I'm here for you," Sato said, "but I can't help you if you don't tell me."

Aoi sighed. "They asked me to leave."

"What?"

"I got there, and my throat hurt so much I had to keep on drinking my water. Then I started coughing, and the producer said it would be a bigger pain to edit me out and told me go home."

Sato stopped.

Aoi's bottom lip trembled, and Sato's heart clenched.

"I'm so sorry that happened," Sato said.

"I need a day or two to recover, and then I'll be fine." Aoi rubbed his eyes.

"You've said that for a while now though." Sato pressed his lips together.

Aoi looked away.

Maybe Sato had gone too far, but he wanted Aoi better. "Maybe it's time to see a doctor."

"I don't know."

"But you said it's been hurting for a while now."

"It's a head cold or allergies."

Sato sighed, wanting to reach out and embrace Aoi, but on the crowded streets it was impossible. Still, the pain in Aoi's eyes said that he was downplaying how much his voice hurt. Sato didn't want to push the issue, but he didn't want to see Aoi make himself suffer unnecessarily.

"I'm here for you. Tell me what you need and I'll do anything."

JANUARY

THE TRAIN DOOR SHUT a few feet before Sato. His train pulled away. He'd missed it by a few seconds, and the next one wasn't scheduled for another fifteen minutes.

He sighed and pulled his phone out of his pocket.

Missed the train. I'll be a little late, Sato texted.

:P More food for me, then, Aoi replied.

He always made that threat, but Sato had always come home to his dinner untouched on the stove. Sato's heart stilled like a packed commuter train during rush hour. Today had been his first day returning to the office since the New Year holiday. It also was Aoi's first time home alone since his doctor ordered him on vocal rest a few weeks back. He'd be spending six whole weeks not uttering a single word.

Their New Year's celebrations flowed in a steady silence. They'd skipped visiting Sato's parents. Aoi had even skipped out on Jin's New Year's orphan party. It had provided Sato a small relief. He'd always feared Aoi would realize how boring he was compared to the rock stars that surrounded Jin. It was silly to think such things, but it still happened the later the night grew when Aoi went out with his friends.

They'd spent the holiday watching anime, which allowed for Aoi's silence, but Sato had missed the playful banter they usually shared.

Sato pushed the thoughts of New Year's behind him and strolled to a bookstore in the station. Hundreds of books with red sale stickers lined the shelves. Prices had been slashed to almost nothing, in keeping with the superstition about holding on to old stock after New Year's.

Glossy cookbooks filled one section. Sato ran his fingers over the covers until he landed on one about traditional Japanese cooking, Aoi's favorite. He opened to one with a yummy-looking bento box on the cover and flipped through the pages, each filled with more delicious-looking dishes. Aoi had made a few of them before, but most were things Sato had never tried. Aoi usually didn't go by a recipe when he cooked, but he'd probably get bored sitting at home all day. He could always change up the recipe if he wanted.

The rest of the store didn't have too much of anything outside of popular novels and nonfiction books. It wasn't like the train station close to home, where the shelves were lined with manga. The magazines might've had something interesting to kill time on the train. He scanned the titles and headlines then stopped.

Aoi was on the cover of one of the gossip magazines with the kanji for "missing" underneath it. Sato curled his fingers.

Aoi had told his agent to cancel his TV appearances and not allow them to announce why. Aoi had feared people would think his voice was messed up even after he recovered. Of course the rumors would start.

Sato groaned and snatched the magazine and flipped to the page with the small story about Aoi. Most of it was questions and vague rumors people had heard. Aoi had joined the secret recording of the *Wild Skies* anime, he'd joined a gay cult, or he and his boyfriend had eloped and were having a long honeymoon in Hawaii.

Sato sighed.

Definitely not that one.

He put the magazine back. It wasn't worth getting worked up about silly rumors or bringing them to Aoi's attention so he'd worry more.

"I'M HOME," SATO called out.

He didn't get a reply, of course.

A delicious smell of something from their small kitchen made Sato's stomach grumble. He stepped into the freezing apartment, not bothering to take off his coat. Aoi wore a blanket cloaked over him as he sat at the low kotatsu table, refusing to put on the space heater, like usual. Their goldfish, Nightingale, joined him. Her tank blocked by volumes of the *Wild Skies* manga. He must've been bored if he was reading Sato's Gundam collection.

"You can use the space heater as well as the kotatsu, you know." Sato clicked on the standing unit, then sat.

How was your day? Aoi held up a whiteboard with the message scrawled on it.

"It was fine," Sato said. "I got you a gift."

Aoi pursed his lips and wiped the board clean. He grabbed the marker and wrote, *I hope it wasn't expensive.*

"It was on sale."

Still.

"Think of it as an extra New Year's gift." Sato held out the package for Aoi.

He gave Sato a stare that spoke volumes before grabbing the package. Aoi carefully tore it open. His eyes grew wide, and he hugged the book. All his movements had become exaggerated since the start of his vocal rest, like Aoi had become more like the anime characters he'd played. It was cute.

He tugged on Sato's tie until he bent down low enough to give him a quick kiss.

"Good, I'm glad you like it," Sato said. "I figured you might want to try something new. You gotta be bored if you're reading my manga."

I wanted to see why you liked it so much.

"Ah, so do you like it?"

It's okay.

Sato laughed.

There should be more kissing.

"Hiro and Hitome kiss."

Aoi scrunched his face and wrote, *No, there should be more of the guys kissing each other.*

"You know it's not that kind of manga."

Aoi let out a dramatic sigh.

"What smells so good? I'm hungry."

I made curry bread with egg, Aoi wrote.

"Eh? Really? You made the bread from scratch too?"

Aoi nodded.

"I'm sure it'll be amazing. You got the kanji wrong."

Aoi raised a brow.

"The kanji for cooked egg is like this." Sato grabbed the board and fixed the kanji. "See? I wrote a paper once in college and used the incorrect kanji. My Japanese professor gave a whole lecture about the difference between the two to the whole class. I was so embarrassed."

Aoi took back the board. *Writing everything out is harder than it looks.*

Sato sighed. "I know it's rough, but it's for the best. I do miss hearing you moan. You think moaning counts as talking?"

Aoi hid the board, but a sexy grin grew on his face as he wrote.

Why don't we play a game?

Sato's stomach rumbled, but he knew Aoi's games always left him more satisfied than any meal.

"What kind of game do you have in mind?"

Write out what you want me to do to get you moaning.

Sato took the board and twirled the marker in his fingers as he thought. Somehow writing out all his lascivious thoughts was easier than having to say it after Aoi's playful commands to do so.

Unzip your pants, Sato wrote and held up the board.

Aoi slowly unzipped his jeans tooth by tooth. Sato's skin prickled. He licked his lips and leaned in to kiss Aoi, but Aoi pulled away. He shoved the marker back into Sato's hand, tapped on the board, and grinned.

Sato groaned, snatched the nearby washcloth, and cleared the board. It didn't really clear off the marks so much as lighten them. Sato could still make out the faint "you're going to abandon me tomorrow" Aoi had written the night before.

Let me kiss you, Sato wrote.

Aoi nodded.

Sato slid off his glasses. They would get in the way. Their lips met, and Sato couldn't believe how he'd managed to go so long at work without feeling Aoi's luscious tongue lap at his lips, encouraging him to open his mouth.

It had taken Aoi so long before he'd finally agreed to see a doctor. All the while Sato, could feel the pent-up anxiety anytime Aoi talked. To the doctor, Aoi had confessed that each time he spoke, it had felt like a battle to get the words out. When the doctor had suggested vocal rest, it had come as a relief to Sato, realizing Aoi would be better in a few weeks. Yet as the first few weeks slipped by, Sato had discovered a different unease radiating off Aoi. Since he couldn't work, he wouldn't be able to contribute to the household funds. Sato didn't care, but the lack of income had always been a sticking point for Aoi. Except for New Year's, all their meals were cost-effective. Delicious, but still nothing fancy. Sato wanted to help Aoi forget all of that for a few minutes.

Sato pulled away, using his left hand to caress Aoi's neck as he popped the lid off the marker with his right.

Take off your clothes, he wrote.

Aoi read it and shook his head, grabbing the marker and writing out, *Gotta be more specific*.

He was playing rough.

Sato accepted the new rule and wrote, *Pull your shirt over your head.*

Aoi pushed the blanket off his shoulders and grabbed the end of his shirt. He tugged it slowly up, revealing a slim stomach and hardened sepia nipples from the chill in the air. Sato could devour Aoi right there, but Aoi would've poked him in the ribs with the marker first. He had such cool control even in the heat of passion. It amazed Sato. Aoi waited and tilted his head at Sato.

Take off my coat and tie.

Aoi leaned forward. The sweet scent of his yuzu soap hitting Sato's nose drove him wild. Aoi unhooked the first button of Sato's coat and slowly worked his way down. His fingers lightly ghosted over Sato's shirt, making his toes curl. Aoi pulled it off Sato's shoulders, who helped get out of the sleeves. The tie came next, a simple tugging as Aoi's breath blew hot against Sato's neck. Aoi tossed it to the side and leaned back as if daring Sato to write something scandalous.

Sato wiped the board clean and pulled it close. The font size got a bit smaller as he wrote, but once he was done, he turned it over for Aoi to read.

Take out your cock so I can suck you dry. Pull my hair, as I suck. You can bite at your lip all you want, but when I'm done you'll be moaning.

Sato could've never been able to say the words without turning redder than the Crimson Knight Rider Gundam, but writing them out gave him a newfound dominance, or maybe he was copying what he remembered reading from one of Aoi's gay romance novels. Either way, the grin on Aoi's face was met with approval.

Aoi took his half-hard cock out of his jeans and leaned back on his hands to welcome Sato's mouth. His tongue grew thick and heavy in his mouth. He grabbed ahold of Aoi's cock and hummed as he took it in.

Aoi's legs opened, struggling against the fabric of the jeans. His fingers made their way into Sato's hair and tugged, encouraging each slurp to go further. And Sato loved each minute of it. He wanted to engulf all of Aoi.

Sato buried himself in the rough fabric, and he looked up to see Aoi biting his lower lip. It only encouraged Sato to pull Aoi out of his mouth and suck on the tip. He ran his tongue along the slit before swallowing all of it again. He repeated it over and over, his tongue drawing new angles of pleasing attack each time.

He wanted Aoi to feel good, to forget even for a few minutes everything with his voice.

Aoi's fingers flinched as if silently telling Sato he was about to cum. Sato dove deep and took in all of Aoi, humming at the back of his throat and milking him for everything he was worth.

Aoi came in a soft moan.

Sato let Aoi's length slip out of his mouth, and he smiled. Aoi wrapped his arms around Sato and gave him a deep kiss. When they parted, Aoi took the board back.

Thank you for helping me forget, Aoi wrote.

Sato grinned and took the pen. *Who said we were finished?*

FEBRUARY

"WHY DO YOU KEEP on pacing?" Aoi said.

"I hate it when doctors are late." Sato continued to pace the small room. "They get mad when you're late, but we were in the waiting room half an hour and we've been in here for fifteen."

Aoi's fingers curled around the examining table he sat on. The lines in Sato's forehead deepened. Aoi had never seen him so angry before. He'd always been the reserved one. The model throat on the counter squeezed his own tighter. He looked away, but it didn't help his queasy stomach. Each wall of the room was covered in something throat related. He jiggled his foot as he waited.

"Thanks for taking the day off to come with me."

"Of course I'd take the day off. I'm here for you whenever you need me."

"Then can you sit down? You're making me nervous."

Sato pushed up his glasses. "Sorry. The waiting gets to me."

"Then read something."

Aoi hopped off the table and grabbed one of the magazines from the stack hanging by the door. It wasn't a Gundam manga, but it would have to do.

"Sorry." Sato thumbed through one of the magazines.

"It's okay."

Six weeks of complete silence had turned into an exhausting chore. Sure, he and Sato had some fun write-your-own-porn nights, but having to keep quiet during the whole encounter was too one-sided for a man who'd spent his life perfecting his moans. The day Aoi had finally started talking was fine, but after a week, his conversations had crept back into the shallow, breathy pain of pushing out each word. It was like he hadn't been on vocal rest at all.

Aoi's foot banged against the metal table, the sound echoing around the room. He'd canceled so many events his agent had booked for after the rest. She might've enjoyed how the rumor magazines still kept him in the news, but if he didn't start work again, he'd fade into obscurity. It would be like resetting his career from the beginning.

The doctor knocked before entering. He was an older gentleman with gray hair and glasses that were the height of fashion in the eighties.

"Aoi Hirayama?"

"Present." Aoi raised his hand.

Was he back in school? His stomach shouldn't be flopping like he'd forgotten to study for an exam. The doctor was there to help.

The doctor glanced toward Sato. "And this is?"

"A friend. It's okay for him to stay, right?"

"Of course." The doctor pulled up a wheeled stool and thumbed through Aoi's file. "Last time you were here, I recommended vocal rest."

Aoi nodded.

"How did that go?"

"It was hard, but I didn't say a single word."

"The voice feeling better?"

Even thinking about speaking scratched his throat. "It still feels off."

Sato raised an eyebrow. "Still?"

Aoi bit his lip. He hadn't exactly told Sato his voice felt the same.

The doctor stood, grabbed a tongue depressor, and told Aoi to open his mouth. Aoi closed his eyes, following the doctor's instructions to make sounds, feeling the same pain. Aoi knew the next step even if he hadn't wanted to think about it. He'd put all his hopes on the vocal rest.

"Explain how it feels?" The doctor pulled away.

Aoi rubbed his throat. "It feels harder than it should."

"The next move after vocal rest is surgery. That might be what is necessary to get your voice back to normal."

"Might!" Sato stood. "But you told him vocal rest would do the trick."

"Sato, sit down," Aoi said.

"After a long vocal rest, most people are back to normal."

Sato crossed his arms. "This is unacceptable. You had him thinking he'd be fine in six weeks."

"Go outside and wait for me there, Sato!" It came out harsher than he wanted, but it worked.

Sato's face flushed red, and he bowed his head and left. The door slammed shut behind him, and the doctor cleared his throat.

"Sorry about that," Aoi said.

"No worries. Everyone is a little different. I can understand getting frustrated."

"Can we talk about what you can do for my voice?"

"Let me pull up your laryngoscopy video."

Aoi nodded, but the image of his marred vocal cords had haunted him in his sleep all during the vocal rest. In a few clicks, the video footage was no longer memory but there in front of him. A fleshy red bump surrounded his white vocal cords on both sides of his throat. The left side was disgustingly swollen, with hard white dots on the opposite side.

"You've got these two nasty polyps here. I think this one right on your folds is even making a callus on the other side. It keeps hitting back and forth when you talk, so it's bound to cause some damage. See here." He played the video. "Every time you speak, the larger polyp is blocking you from closing the folds all the way. It's like you have to work doubly hard to get the words out."

Aoi nodded. "That accounts for the breathiness. I feel like every time I speak, I have to force it out."

"These polyps happen and do nasty things to your voice. You've been feeling the results."

"Did the vocal rest shrink them? Like I need to do another few weeks?"

"I would have to do another laryngoscopy to see, but to be honest, like I told you the first time we looked at this video, I think surgery is the best way to go."

Aoi pressed his lips together and leaned away from the doctor. It had been true, but the thought of a sharp, pointy knife coming at his cords sent him into a bottomless panic. "Isn't there medication I can take?"

"There isn't."

"Surgery is the only way?"

"I can show you videos of someone with similar polyps if you'd like to get a better idea."

"Sure."

More clicks and the doctor explained how the surgery was a few simple snips.

"After surgery, you have a few days of vocal rest, then some therapy, and you should be back to normal."

Aoi's eyes narrowed. "Another 'should'?"

"Any kind of operation on the vocal cords can cause some alteration. I can't guarantee that your voice will sound exactly the same."

His stomach churned, and he wished Sato was there so he could clutch onto him. Aoi curled his fingers around his arm. His voice was his life. He couldn't throw it all away on something without a guarantee.

Aoi bit his lip. "It's basically surgery or my voice will stay screwed?"

"If the polyps grow bigger, it might get worse."

Aoi winced and clutched himself tighter. Even if he let them butcher his voice box, it might come back.

"After surgery, how many people are back to normal?" he asked.

"Almost all, ninety-eight percent." The doctor stood and looked down at Aoi. "You're a voice actor, right? So this surgery is like if you were an athlete and you injured your leg. You wouldn't hesitate about getting the surgery. We can schedule it in a few weeks."

Aoi chewed on his bottom lip. "I think I need more time to think about it first."

"Sure. Call me back when you're ready."

The doctor left, and Aoi stared at one of the throat posters. He couldn't take a chance and screw up his voice. It had got him out of homelessness. It was everything he had and the only thing no one could take away from him. But with the way things were, he'd never be a main character again. If it got worse, he'd be stuck working at a convenience store again. Roadie life paid more, but he didn't want to abandon Sato.

Aoi left the room and went back to the front office. Sato stood up and walked over.

"I'm sorry," Sato said. "I didn't mean to embarrass you. I was just mad."

"I'm pissed it didn't work too. Let's get out of here."

They walked to the elevator, and as soon as the door shut, Aoi wrapped his arms around Sato and kissed him, finally getting the closeness he craved. He pulled away when it dinged.

"I don't know what to do," Aoi said.

Sato squeezed Aoi's hand. "Only do the surgery if you feel comfortable, but your voice is everything. It's like how I wear glasses to make my eyesight better."

Aoi rubbed his throat and could almost feel the ugly polyps sticking out. How could something he used every day betray him so much?

MARCH

AOI STIRRED THE SIMMERING pot of soup and double-checked the recipe to make sure he'd added everything. He'd never follow the recipe, but everything in the cookbook Sato had given him proved delicious without much modification. Trying a new one every few days had given him some entertainment between reading over fan mail begging him for news about his return.

A knock on the door dragged Aoi's attention away from the food.

Aoi opened the door.

"It's been forever," Jin said.

"I wasn't the one on tour for two months."

"Gotta jump when the manager tells us."

They hugged, and both Aoi's and Jin's blond hair could've come from the same bottle of bleach. They'd both be considered short, but Jin was tall enough he could rub his extra centimeter in Aoi's face. Jin leaned down and pulled up the six-pack he'd set down.

"Survivors." Jin handed the six-pack to Aoi.

He pulled one of the bottles from the container—a brew from Sapporo. All the other bottles were from different cities Jin's band had stopped at on the tour.

"Thanks. Which one's the best?" Aoi asked.

"I liked the Osaka, but Kazuki liked the Kyoto."

Aoi nodded, taking the Osaka one and sticking the rest in the fridge.

"What smells so good?" Jin wandered inside and took off his pointy-toed boots.

"Dinner tonight for Sato and me."

Jin grabbed a spoon off the stove and took a taste. He closed his eyes and licked his lips.

"Are you sure I can't stay?"

"Three's a crowd."

"But there's so much food. You're going all out, aren't you?"

Aoi shrugged. "I had all day after my run. I know it's yours and Kazuki's White Day too, so thanks for coming for a chat."

"No worries. I saw his pierced face all day on tour, so it's good. We were going to meet up at his place for dinner."

"I didn't know Kazuki liked to cook."

"We're getting takeout, then getting drunk and trying out a new sex toy."

Aoi covered his ears. "Too much information."

"It's going to be this new harness. Supposed to go over the bed."

"I'm not listening."

Jin laughed. "Are you saying you and Sato haven't added any toys?"

"Even if we did, I'm not telling you."

"Vanilla." Jin playfully stuck out his tongue, then plopped down beside the kotatsu. "But I guess Sato is a salaryman."

Aoi had missed the playful joking when Jin was away. Aoi took a swig of the beer, a nice bold flavor. He tried not to catch a glimpse of the scripts strewn in mountains on the table, but it was impossible.

"I know who's to blame for why all your lyrics are nothing but thinly veiled allusions to sex."

Jin laughed, and Aoi joined in.

"The tour went well?" Aoi asked.

"We sold out the Budokan arena. They filmed it. You'll have the buy the special-edition Blu-ray since you missed it."

"I would want to scream like everyone else. My voice couldn't handle it. Next thing you'll be selling out the Tokyo Dome."

"You'll have to come when we sell out the Tokyo Dome."

"Really? You sold out there?"

"I can dream, right?" Jin flipped through one of the scripts on the table. "What did you want to talk about? You finally asking Sato to marry you?"

Aoi spit out his beer. "What! Where did you get that idea?"

"You've been living together for so long. It's the logical next step." Jin shrugged. "Screw the government if they won't fully recognize it."

Aoi rubbed his thumb over the beer label. He and Sato had been living together for years. Aoi couldn't imagine being with anyone else. Still… It didn't seem like much of a point if it wouldn't be accepted everywhere.

"Remember I told you about going to go to the doctor for my voice?" Aoi said.

"You did that vocal rest thing. Did that work?"

"No."

"Oh."

"I had my follow-up appointment two weeks ago, and he suggested I have surgery."

Jin nodded. "When are you scheduled?"

Aoi squeezed the beer a little tighter, condensation slicking his hand. "I haven't decided if I'm doing it yet. I wanted to talk to you first."

"What? Why? You have Sato to talk about stuff like this with."

"He wouldn't understand. His livelihood doesn't depend on his voice."

"Exactly. So what are you waiting for?" Jin pointed to the stack of scripts. "They'll get someone else to voice-act these if you don't."

Aoi sighed. "I thought if I expanded to roles outside of BL they'd give me minor roles. My voice should've been able to handle those, but everything my agent sent, they wanted me for the lead."

"You've become the biggest gay icon there is—of course no one wants you for minor roles."

Aoi ran his fingers through his hair. Why wasn't Jin understanding? It wasn't as easy as a little snip and everything would be perfect.

"And you can't go back to small roles. That's going backwards."

"And then my agent sent me this." Aoi dug through the scripts and pulled out one for the *Wild Skies* Gundam series. "Look, it's Sato's favorite."

"Doesn't he like all the Gundam?"

"He does, but this one is different. Critiques think it's going to turn *Evangelion* huge once they finally get the anime made. All the manga fans are nuts about it, and everyone will know it when it comes out."

"So you'd be stupid to pass it up."

"Exactly." Aoi's shoulders slumped. "But I know with the voice I have now, it won't hold up for a series. My agent said they'd been thinking of me for this role all along. If I accept an audition, then I pretty much have it in the bag, but I would have to disclose how jacked up my voice is."

"What are you waiting for, then?"

"They'll make me wait until after I recover to go through a second audition before they make a formal offer."

"Then you have the surgery and be fine. I don't get what you're asking me."

Aoi took a deep breath and stared at the script. How could Jin not connect the dots? He depended on his voice for his livelihood like him.

"The doctor might screw up, and my career will be gone," Aoi whispered, squeezing out the secret locked inside.

"It'll be gone if you can't voice-act anything but minor roles too."

"You understand though, don't you? If it was you and your voice was on the line, what would you do?"

Jin stared at Aoi like he was insane. How could he not see that going under the knife meant he was trusting his future to the hands of someone else? He couldn't even trust his parents with it.

"I would have the surgery," he said. "Many vocalists have gotten polyps removed, and they were fine. Kyo and Ryu, they were out for a few months but then back to recording."

Aoi shook his head. "But what about Navi? She had hers removed, and it didn't help. She had to quit and start some online design site."

"What is it that you're really afraid of?"

"That my voice will be fucked up."

Jin leaned forward. "I've known you long enough that I can tell it's not that."

Aoi's heart twisted like a well-worn script. "I don't want to go back."

"Come on." Jin squeezed Aoi's shoulder. "It won't go backwards. You have Sato now, and there was a time when every month I would see your face on a dozen magazine covers. On the very slim chance the surgery doesn't work, you'll never have to worry about finding somewhere to work. I mean, you see this stack of scripts. Even if you stick to minor roles, people still want you."

Aoi pressed his lips together.

"Ask Sato if you don't believe me, but he'll tell you the same."

"He's going to be home soon." Aoi stood. "Want me to show you how to make the tempura?"

Jin stared at him with one of those looks that told Aoi his change of subject wasn't very good, but Jin wasn't getting it. The very thought of someone cutting away at his throat sent his heart pounding. If Jin didn't understand, there was no way Sato could imagine the terror.

"Tempura sounds good," Jin finally said. "Maybe we'll do that instead of takeout."

"Don't catch the apartment on fire."

During the instructions, Aoi had to stop and take big gulps of water to keep the strain in his voice from aching. Yet Jin's lecture nagged at his insides. Aoi couldn't keep hiding from his fans. He'd gotten so many concerned letters during Valentine's Day that he had to stop reading them. Sure, day-to-day talking was okay, but he didn't want to live like that. He didn't want to miss out on Jin's next big concert because he couldn't resist cheering for them during the show.

"I'm home," Sato called out.

"Welcome home," Jin and Aoi said in unison.

Sato walked over and took a gulp of Aoi's beer. "Did the tour go well?"

"It was awesome. You'll see it when Aoi buys the super-special edited Blu-ray in a few months."

Aoi laughed. "I guess my days of free swag are gone."

"Yup. I should get going." Jin snatched a few more tempura green beans, then left.

Aoi finished the last batch of vegetables while Sato undid his tie and put his jacket in the closet.

"Does everything taste as good as it smells?" Sato asked.

"It's better since I spent all day on it."

Aoi gave Sato a peck on the cheek before they brought the tempura to the table. They shoved Aoi's scripts off to one side and sat beside each other.

"You found one you can do yet?" Sato asked.

"Actually, I was thinking about going for this one." Aoi pulled out the script for *Wild Skies* and handed it to Sato. It was why he'd made such a big meal.

His eyes grew wide. "The rumors are true! They are making it into an anime."

"It's still kind of on the down-low, so don't tell anyone, or I'll get in trouble. They want me to play Hiro, and I still have to do a formal audition, but it's pretty clear they want me."

"That's so amazing!" Sato flipped through the script, and then his smile faded. "He's one of the main characters, and Gundam series are usually long. Are you going to be okay?"

Aoi took in a deep breath and intertwined his and Sato's fingers. He had no choice even if the very thought of it terrified him. But Sato was there. He'd be the rock he needed.

"I think I'm going to go ahead with the surgery," Aoi said.

"You're not doing this because of how much I love this anime, are you?"

"Even talking for a few minutes straight hurts. I've been kind of downplaying how bad it was this whole time."

"Why would you do that?" The pain in Sato's voice ripped through Aoi's heart.

"I'm sorry. I couldn't bring myself to admit how bad it was. I was lying to myself, but that made it so I was lying to you."

"But that means you did all that worrying by yourself. We're a couple, aren't we? That means we worry about things together."

Sato leaned in, taking Aoi in his arms. The warmth radiating off him made Aoi smile. He could stay forever in Sato's arms.

"I'm sorry," Aoi whispered.

"Tell me you won't keep something like that to yourself again," Sato whispered.

Aoi closed his eyes and clutched Sato tighter. "I won't."

APRIL

SATO PUSHED UP HIS glasses and reread the notes he'd taken during the meeting with the lawyer. Sato had scribbled everything so fast that some of the words slurred together.

"You need to sign this too." Sato twirled the pen between his fingers.

"I didn't think there would be this much paperwork." Aoi walked over and signed the paper.

"We need to cover every possibility."

"But it's so unfair."

Sato pressed his lips together. The whole thing weighed down on him. He wanted to scream out all his frustrations, but even after there was nothing he could do and the weight of Aoi's surgery pulled them down enough.

"I mean, I get why we're doing it," Aoi said, "but a straight couple wouldn't have to do any of this shit, but we had to hire a lawyer to make sure we fill out the right paperwork. Then go back to get it all official. And all of this is just in case I have to stay overnight at the hospital so you could legally visit me."

Sato squeezed Aoi's arm. "Once we get them signed, we won't have to do it again. It'll cover both of us in case anything happens."

Aoi nodded, but the circles under his eyes looked darker by the day. Sato pushed himself away from the desk.

"Come here," he said.

Sato wrapped his arms around Aoi, pulling him onto his lap. Aoi let out a small moan, and Sato kissed his neck.

"You sleeping okay?" Sato asked.

"Yeah."

He wished Aoi wouldn't lie, but it was his way of not making Sato worry, which made it worse. Still, with all the documents they were signing, he'd figured Aoi would've gotten the hint that he was in it for the long haul. Sato's hand slipped underneath Aoi's shirt.

"You sure?" Sato asked, hoping the extra push would lead Aoi to a more truthful answer.

"It's okay."

"You still have a few weeks before the surgery. Maybe see if there's a marathon coming up or join a running club. It might help you get your mind off things."

"But I haven't been training for a marathon. Starting to train now won't work."

"You do them for the fun of it anyway. Or you could see if Jin will let you hang out with the band as they record songs."

"Maybe," Aoi mumbled.

Sato held on to Aoi a little tighter. Hopefully he'd be back to his normal bubbly self once the surgery was over with.

They stayed quiet, with Aoi leaning back against Sato and clutching his hand.

The unease faded though once Aoi thumbed through the stack of paperwork they hadn't gotten to.

"I feel like you could have gotten a degree in law with the amount of research you ended up putting in for this," Aoi said.

Sato laughed. "You didn't want to spend any more time than necessary in that lawyer's office. So I had to know exactly what to ask."

"You saw how much he charged per half hour. We walked out of there and I almost died at the bill. It's worth it, sure, but yikes."

Sato gave Aoi's hand a light squeeze, trying to put every-thing he wasn't saying into the small gesture. "Remember, we only have to do it once."

Aoi ran his fingers through his hair. "I know."

"The wills are next in the stack. Who do you want getting your manga?"

"Everything gets more morbid the deeper we go into that stack."

"Everyone has to make a will sometime. So at least it's not something special since we're together."

"I might as well ask for something bad to happen on the operating table."

"Aoi."

Sato couldn't watch as Aoi's nerves grew more and more frazzled by the day. He'd stopped running, saying that when he did, he could only think of the surgical scissors cutting at his vocal cords, and yesterday he'd forgot to turn the stove on when he was cooking. He'd spent ten minutes waiting for the butter to melt. He'd passed it off as forgetfulness, but Sato could see through the lie. Watching such a strong person as Aoi drove Sato to become better. He didn't know how, but he'd keep trying.

"You'll be fine," Sato whispered, kissing Aoi's neck. "The doctor has a lot of experience, and you'll be back to moaning at full capacity soon."

Aoi half laughed. "That'll be nice."

Sato's hand trailed down the outside of Aoi's thigh. "I can't tell you how much I've missed them."

A knock on the door, and Sato narrowed his eyes. A guest would intervene in his perfect plan to distract Aoi from everything by having sexy time.

"Did you invite Jin over?" he asked.

Aoi shook his head and got up. The knock came again as Aoi strolled over. His ass always looked pinchable in those jeans.

"Surprise!" Michiko's voice scratched at his eardrums as the door opened. She was the last person he needed dropping by unexpectedly.

"What are you doing here?" Sato asked.

"Can't I visit my brother and his boyfriend? I brought a cake to celebrate Aoi's path to recovery."

"I haven't had the surgery yet."

"But deciding to have it is the first step."

She embraced Aoi, standing more than a head taller than him as her flowing pink chiffon dress swallowed him up. They'd gotten so close over the mutual love of BL.

"What kind of cake is it?" Aoi asked.

"You'll have to see to find out."

Sato rubbed his forehead. "I thought we had a talk about appropriate surprises when you gave Aoi his birthday present last year."

"You blow everything I do out of proportion."

"You gave him heart-shaped anal beads in front of our parents."

"It's not like they'd know what they were."

Sato glared at her. He didn't know why he tried, because it never worked. She floated across the vestibule with a lavender-colored cake box with a cartoon bee on the side. She gently placed the cake on the kotatsu before plopping down like a pink fog.

"It took me forever to find one that would agree to the design," she said.

It couldn't be good. Sato swore the prime minister had strengthened the obscenity laws because of his sister.

Sato stood and slowly walked over to them. From what he could see from the clear windows on the top, the cake wasn't shaped like a huge dick, so that was a plus. Yet as Michiko pulled it out of the cake box, he understood why she had to go to several bakeries. A dozen chibi anime-styled characters were drawn on the cake. Some were sweet with kissing, and others...

"Are those five guys having an orgy?" Aoi's tone cheered the cake's praise.

"Yes!" She jumped. "Take a closer look."

Sure, all the major parts where hidden by conveniently placed hands and legs, but it was clear what was going on. Only his sister would think a porno cake would be an appropriate gift.

"Wait." Aoi cocked his head. "These are all characters I voice-acted."

"Exactly. What better way to celebrate your voice? It's a lemon and poppy-seed cake."

"Yummy."

Sato crossed his arms. "Really, Michiko. You made some poor baker draw that for you?"

"He said he was a fan of Aoi's work too. So he didn't mind one bit."

"Most people mellow out their obsession when they get older, but you've gotten worse."

"Like you and your Gundams?" Aoi held up his hand, gesturing to all the figures.

"You're supposed to be on my side."

"You do have a lot, and the cake is pretty cute. I'll get us some plates."

Sato's shoulders finally felt like they could relax with the glow of Aoi's happy-go-lucky self returning.

"I didn't put that Gundam guy you're doing since it's not official yet."

"They're waiting to announce after the surgery. Clearly they want to be able to back out if my voice gets screwed up."

And depressed Aoi was back.

"That'd be stupid if they did," Michiko said. "You and the other lead Kayu were meant for each other. He's so cute, and it would make the perfect enemies-to-lovers plot."

"No, no." Sato passed out the plates. "If Aoi gets shipped with anyone, it should be me. His loving boyfriend for many years now."

"Nah." Michiko shook her head. "Aoi, you're perfect for the role. The underlying theme will have all the fujoshi on the edge wondering when you guys kiss."

"We don't kiss."

"There'll be enough fan art out there everyone will think they did."

Aoi cut through two of the characters' heads while slicing up the first cake piece. Soon, the other ones were in dismembered body parts.

Michiko grabbed the *Wild Skies* manga off the table.

"Why are you touching my things?" Sato said.

"I'm going to show you why Hiro and Kayu would make a good couple."

Aoi laughed. "That settles it. Michiko can have all my manga, and you can have everything else when I die."

Michiko raised an eyebrow. "What's that for?"

"Sato has us filling out all this paperwork that says we can legally make decisions for the other in case something happens." Aoi let out a sigh and shoved a piece of cake in his mouth. "We were on wills when you showed up."

Sato stabbed his fork through one of the characters' arms. "It's sad we have to get one, but it's for the best."

"I swear it would be easier if we got married," Aoi mumbled.

Sato's heart thumped in his chest, and he stared at Aoi. He let out a nervous laugh.

"It probably doesn't matter," Aoi quickly added. "Most of Japan doesn't accept it, and we'd have to still do all the paperwork anyway."

"Here!" Michiko opened the manga to show them both the images. "Here would be a good scene where Hiro and Kayu could fuck. I can write what happens, and you have to say it, right?"

Aoi laughed, but Sato shook his head.

"Michiko, stop ruining my fun of having Aoi voice-act in an anime I like."

"Maybe I'll have to write some alternative-universe fan fiction with you and me both in it," Aoi said.

Sato smiled. It was good to have his Aoi back.

APRIL BONUS

"**T**O AOI'S QUICK RECOVERY!"

Everyone clinked their beers together, then drank. Jin and Kazuki had joined Aoi in his day drinking a few hours earlier, and Sato and Jiro met them at the Gundam-themed bar after work. The two matched well with the rest of the salarymen in the bar, while Jin and Kazuki looked like they'd walked out of a *SHOXX* music magazine.

Aoi took a small sip to maintain the steady buzz through the day. He knew better than to get shitfaced before the surgery even if he wanted to.

Another toast. This one to Aoi's surgeon, who was going to do an amazing job.

Jin and Kazuki were having their own contest of who could chug down the beer the fastest. It was almost sickening how much they looked like they belonged together. It had taken Jin way too long to accept Kazuki's feelings for him.

Jin slammed his glass down and threw his arms up in victory. "Your voice is going to sound so good."

"We'll have to make a new song with him moaning in it again," Kazuki said.

"Your new label probably won't allow it."

"They let me keep these." Kazuki tapped his plethora of lip piercings. "I don't see why a guy moaning would have them worried about censors. Aoi's so popular now they'll probably encourage it."

Jiro leaned forward, eyes wide and locked on Kazuki's piercings. "Did those hurt?"

"When this one got infected, it hurt like a bitch."

Jiro grimaced. "How did they do that?"

Sato's hand tickled Aoi's outer thigh. Aoi smiled even though his stomach sloshed and tumbled. Maybe drinking all day before surgery wasn't the best idea, but it kept him from burying his head underneath his pillow all day.

Sato leaned into Aoi's ear. "Another moaning song sounds perfect."

"You like hearing me."

"With the drama CDs, there's always someone else, but in the song, it's only you."

"Maybe I'll have to drag you into the booth to join me."

"No one wants to hear my moaning."

Aoi propped his chin on his arm. "I always want to hear your moans."

Sato vibrated. Not from Aoi's flirtation, but from the timer on his phone.

"It's midnight." Sato clicked off the alarm.

Aoi sighed and shoved his half-empty beer to Sato.

"How long is it going to take?" Kazuki asked.

"About an hour or so," Aoi said. "But recovery is three weeks. My voice shouldn't sound weak after that."

Jin slapped him on the back. "You'll be fine. Ready to moan out monologues and everything."

Jiro asked Kazuki another question about piercings, which had him talking with the same vigor Sato would about Gundam. The conversation drew on as he went on about the finer details of what needles were used and where else he had holes put in. He'd been put through so much poking and prodding. Like Aoi was going to have with surgery.

He could almost feel the knife poking at his neck. Okay, so the doctor wasn't really cutting into his throat. He'd have some scissors down his throat to cut off the grotesque blobs. Aoi ran his fingers through his hair and groaned.

He stood. "I'm gonna take a leak."

The bathroom resembled one from some mech anime. They blurred together, but Sato would've known.

Aoi pissed while a picture of some lady pilot with big boobs stared at him. The door opened, and Jin strolled in, taking the urinal next to him.

"You okay?" he asked.

"Just taking a piss."

"You usually come in bathrooms to hide."

"Not always."

"Like the time on tour and you forgot to get more stage blood. You hid in the bathroom all during the performance, thinking we'd fire you or something."

"Well, no hiding, just pissing."

Jin laughed and washed his hands. "You know the whole band is cheering you on. They wanted to come, but I stopped them since I know you can't really talk."

"Thanks." Aoi flushed and joined him at the sink. "And thanks for spending the day with me."

The door swung open, and Sato entered. His eyebrows drew together, and a look so worried was plastered on his face it was like Aoi couldn't piss without turning his insides out. He needed to think of a new place to go when he needed to escape, or else he'd have everyone in the bathroom pretending they needed to go.

"I had to use the bathroom," Aoi said. "That's all."

"Oh no. I just—I had to go too," Sato said.

Jin grinned and mouthed an *I told you* before leaving.

Aoi leaned against the sink while Sato peed barely enough to even consider calling it that. Aoi wasn't sure what was worse: the fact that he was hiding in the bathroom or that Sato would always follow him inside.

He couldn't blame them for thinking he was upset. He'd spent the whole day avoiding it by getting drunk.

"We want to go?" Sato's smile hit Aoi's heart like a beam of glowing joy.

"Might as well."

OUT OF ALL the stupid ideas Aoi ever had, going home was one of the biggest. He should've stayed out all night and staggered into the surgery plastered and passed out on the operating table.

He lost count of the minutes… hours he'd spent staring up at the ceiling or at Nightingale swimming around in her tank. Sometimes he thought he'd drifted off to sleep, but he'd wake up from a horrifying nightmare of a pissed-off manga fan complaining about how the anime didn't do it right. How Aoi's voice for Hiro was horrible.

In a few hours he'd be asleep without control, without any say as the doctor sliced into his throat, without knowing the untold amount of damage he'd do until it was too late.

His heart constricted, squeezing his ribs and welling up his eyes. Sato slept beside him. Aoi shouldn't disturb him. He didn't need to burden his lover with one more minute of his inadequacy.

He slipped out of bed and into the bathroom.

His heart grew heavier, each pound lunging into his ribs like the drums beating out one of Lilith's metal songs.

He was going to end up back on the streets. His voice had got him out of it, so without it he'd return.

The tears welled up, streaking his cheeks. A shrieking grasp left his throat.

He didn't want the risk. What if something happened? Michiko would get his manga, Sato everything else. Would his parents even care? He was already dead to them.

He slid down the bathroom wall, trying to muffle his cries with his hand. Even crying hurt his voice. He wiped his eyes, but another sob came.

"Aoi." Sato knocked on the door then turned the knob, but it was locked.

Aoi froze, keeping silent. If he stayed silent, maybe Sato would go away. He bit his lip. He should've gone outside to cry. He should've gotten dressed and hid in a convenience store bathroom. He should've gone anywhere.

"Yeah." Aoi's voice cracked.

"Unlock the door."

"I'm fine."

"You don't sound fine."

"Go back to sleep."

Sato jiggled the handle. "Please, open the door."

"I'm fine."

"Aoi."

He waited, hoping Sato would leave, pretend he'd dreamed up the whole thing.

Aoi stared at the knob a second, willing Sato to leave him alone, but then it turned. Sato wouldn't leave. He was too good to leave. Aoi swallowed and stood. He staggered the few steps and opened the door a crack.

"I'm fine," Aoi said.

Sato pushed opened the door and hugged Aoi, rocking him back and forth. "It'll be all right. I know it's scary."

"But it might not. That's why we filled out all that paperwork."

"It's okay, because we have each other. Your life isn't the same as it was before. My parents will support us too if it comes to it. Michiko will always welcome us with open arms. Even if you'll sneeze because of her cat."

Everything Sato said made sense. Logically Aoi understood, but it didn't stop his heart from crying out, "*Lies.*" Sato's firm embrace smothered it. His hands roamed over his body, distracting him, calling him to think of other things. How much Aoi wanted to go back to thinking of only sheer pleasure.

"It's so hard," Aoi said, unsure if he was talking about the situation or his dick.

"I know."

Even crying, his voice hurt. "Let's go back to bed. I should try to get some sleep."

"Do you want me to get you off? It might help get your mind off things."

Aoi sighed. Moaning hurt, too, or at least the way he wanted to moan for Sato. He'd perfected them. Knew exactly how to purr each deep-throated cry of lust to get Sato's cock stiff in a second. But with his voice jacked up, he couldn't do half of it and ending up biting into his hand to remind himself moaning would be too painful to even attempt.

"I'm not in the mood," Aoi lied.

"We can snuggle, then. It might help get you asleep."

It was worth a try.

SATO GRASPED AOI'S hand, holding it between them. With the way the seats were angled in the waiting room, no one would be able to see the sign of affection. He gave their hands a tight squeeze, and Aoi's jittering leg slowed.

"Why did they tell me to get here so early if they weren't ready?" Aoi mumbled under his breath.

"The doctor can't get his team ready until they know you're here," Sato's mom said.

Sato's whole family had come to support Aoi. Mom, Dad, and even Michiko skipped a day of managing her gym to sit in the waiting room until Aoi was finished. Of course, Aoi hadn't asked for any of it, but Sato knew he needed to be surrounded by people who loved him and would still love him even if his voice worsened.

"Do you remember the time it snowed and you woke me up at the crack of dawn?" Sato asked.

Aoi shook his head. At least it didn't shake as much as his leg.

"I think it was the first snow or something, and we went to the park. It was so early, and no one else was there. You made those two snow bunnies, and I said they were a family." A warmth spread throughout Sato's chest. He squeezed Aoi's hand harder. "Let's do that again the next time it snows. This time we'll have to have five bunnies. One for Mom and Dad, and one for Michiko since they're part of our family too."

Aoi's leg stopped. He looked up at Sato, his eyes glossed over, but not in sadness. He leaned into Sato's shoulder. His shirt dampened from Aoi's tears, and Sato squeezed his hand.

"Thank you," Aoi said.

The door to the back opened, and a nurse called, "Aoi Hirayama."

"We'll be waiting when you get out."

Aoi bit his lip and unlaced his fingers from their bond. Sato knew Aoi would be fine, but he willed all his energy into one last big positive thought for him. His parents wished him well, and then the door shut behind him.

Michiko pulled out a manga from her bag shaped like a cherry blossom. A dark book sock covered the book, probably hiding some scandalous porn underneath. Dad poked around his phone while Mom filled out some puzzle game. Sato had been so worried about how Aoi felt about surgery he'd forgotten to bring something to kill the time. Sure he had his phone, but it was already half dead since he forgot to stick it on the charger.

Sato ran his fingers through his hair. He knew Aoi would be fine, but if he couldn't distract himself, he knew all the doubts Aoi told him would come clawing into his head like unlabeled numbers during tax season.

"You must be Sato," a woman said.

She carried a large box in her hands, and if Michiko's frilly clothes were like a warm spring breeze, hers were a cold winter chill. Black. Serious.

"Yes?" Sato said.

"It's nice to finally meet you. I'm Aoi's agent. He's said good things about you." She plopped the box down in the empty seat beside him and handed Sato her business card. "Did I miss him?"

"By about five minutes."

"Damn. I wanted to give him those. Figured it would help."

"What is it?" Sato asked, already opening the lid.

There had to be at least a thousand notes inside. Some decorated with stickers, others with drawings of little chibi versions of Aoi or the characters he played. There were even some with flowers tied to them with ribbon.

"Since Aoi allowed us to make a statement that he had to withdraw for his health, it opened up the floodgates at our office for his fan mail."

Sato pushed back a layer, exposing more and more drawings and envelopes. "There's so many."

"This is just from today's delivery. Everything else we send over to your apartment. Your office signed for them. I figured it would be good to show him some before going under the knife." She sighed. "But one thing after another. I got called. Everyone wants a comment."

"I see."

If the box was from a day's worth of mail, how many boxes were waiting for them back at their apartment? Aoi had gotten more than enough chocolate for Valentine's Day to keep them in sweets for a year.

"You'll tell him I stopped by."

"Will do."

She gave a curt nod. "The producer wants another vocal test in three weeks when he's better. I'll email him the information when it gets closer."

"Got it."

She left as her phone rang again. She rattled off the generic response that Aoi was away for his health and there was nothing else to report. She waved goodbye to Sato and left.

Sato plopped back in the chair.

"There is a lot of mail," Mom said.

Sato grabbed one of the letters. "Yeah, Aoi has a lot more support than he thinks."

He opened the letter, reading it through. In it, a lady talked about how seeing Aoi coming out on TV had inspired her to come out as bisexual to her parents and that she wished him good health. Another letter detailed how she was a fan for Aoi for so long and that he would continue to have her support. Each letter filled Sato's chest with pride a little more. His boyfriend inspired people.

He'd found the person he wanted to spend the rest of his life with.

AOI PUSHED UP the large sunglasses covering half of his face and entered the Korean restaurant. The chef gave a happy welcome, and Aoi took a stool in the corner of the bar. There were only four other seats, all empty. Aoi purposely picked the off-hour hoping for a peaceful, undisturbed outing, but with the person he extended the invitation to, he doubted it would happen. He ordered green tea and poked around his phone while waiting.

His social media was filled with well wishes from fans. He tried to avoid the rabbit-hole threads filled with people guessing what lethal disease inflicted him. He read enough of happy fan letters dropped off at his apartment to leave him eager to come back to work, but no matter how much his vocal coach said he sounded good, a little voice niggled in his head. And that voice sounded like Atsushi.

Who strolled into the restaurant and pushed his black, shoulder-length hair behind his ear. His silver-and-gray shirt, tight across his chest, was short enough to expose a sliver of skin along his stomach. If he wasn't such a jerk, he would've been hot, but at least he was honest. If Aoi's voice was even a little off, he'd rub it in Aoi's face.

A punchable sly smile spread across Atsushi's face. "If it wasn't for your height, I wouldn't be able to recognize you with those ridiculous sunglasses."

"Shut up."

"Now, now, that's not very nice considering you were the one who called my agent to set up this date."

"It's not a date," Aoi said between clenched teeth.

Atsushi slid onto his stool and leaned close. "It sure looks like a date."

"Fuck you."

"Oh, feisty. I'll pay if that's what you're worried about. I know you've been out of work."

"We're paying for ourselves."

A fire built in Aoi's stomach, telling him how much of a bad idea it was inviting Atsushi out. Yet Aoi would rather hear his voice wasn't back to normal from him than the director of *Wilds Skies*.

They ordered, Atsushi copying Aoi's choice of beef bulgogi.

"So why am I here?" Atsushi asked.

Aoi swallowed, keeping a few seconds of the optimistic bliss of pretending his voice sounded as good as everyone said.

"Can you tell?" Aoi asked.

"That you couldn't resist me?"

"No." Aoi's leg jiggled on the rung of the stool. "My voice. Does it sound different?"

"Hmm." Atsushi tapped his finger to his lips. "I can't really tell. Maybe if I got a picture of us pretending to kiss, then I would be able to tell."

"That's never going to happen."

"It's what the fans want."

"I knew this was a stupid idea." Aoi stood.

Atsushi grabbed Aoi's arm before he could run away. "You went ahead with the surgery."

"Yeah."

Atsushi leaned back, releasing Aoi's arm. "Good."

"So? Can you tell the difference? Is it back to normal?"

"Hard to tell. You've only said a few words to me."

Aoi rubbed his thumb over the rim of his teacup. His stomach clenched. He wasn't sure if it was from the delicious savory scent of cooked beef or that he hated that he needed something from Atsushi so much his stomach decided to eat itself.

"If I talk more, will you tell me if it was a success?"

"If I can't get a picture of us kissing, then I at least want a picture of us eating together."

"You don't get to call it a date."

"Deal."

The chef handed them their order, arranging the side dishes on a shelf in front of them. Atsushi thanked him, flashed the charming smile that made Aoi want to gag, and asked the chef if he'd take their picture.

Atsushi made Aoi take off his glasses and swung his arm around him like they were old friends. He'd scheduled the picture to post on his media accounts until long after they'd be gone, but he stilled linked to Aoi's account and with enough vague emojis that would inspire more than a few fanfics.

Aoi grabbed a piece of the beef bulgogi with the metal chopsticks, and a subtle sweet tang burst over his tongue. Atsushi's company wasn't too bad as they sat there silently eating their lunch. He even let Aoi have all of the mushroom side dish after he'd noticed Aoi enjoyed them so much.

"I won't be able to know if your voice is back unless you talk. Moaning would work too. No other actor I've worked with is even half as good as when you really let loose."

The back of Aoi's neck grew hot. "What do you want me to talk about?"

Atsushi shrugged. "Tell me about your boyfriend."

"You want to know about him?"

"Not really, but you love him, don't you? So, you'll forget about the way you sound and talk. That's the only way I'll be able to tell for sure that your voice is back."

Aoi sighed. He wanted to keep Sato separate from Atsushi. Even talking about him made seem it like he was sharing him with work.

"He's a really nice guy," Aoi said.

"So said everyone who dated anyone. Everyone is nice to someone they like. You need to get specific."

He'd never really talked about Sato with anyone but Jin. Aoi put his chopsticks down and took in a breath. He needed to let go.

"He's a huge geek. He'd probably still be building models while watching old VHS tapes of anime series not released on DVD if we hadn't met. He'd eat nothing but vending machine food because he'd rather spend money on a new model kit. Now we trade off days on what series we watch together. He still blushes at all the sexy scenes in the anime I pick, especially with the stuff I acted in. It's cute watching him pretend to not be fazed, but his whole body is scorching." Aoi sighed. "I really do love him. Like I can feel it throughout my whole body. I couldn't imagine a future without him."

"You've acted in too many romance series." Atsushi propped his head on his hand.

"Well, I was thinking of—"

"All those sappy words sticking in your brain."

Aoi groaned. Of course, more teasing. "So how was my voice?"

"You sounded fine. Maybe even better than when we acted together in that last series." Atsushi leaned forward and pulled Aoi's sunglasses off and slipped them on himself. "You need to start showing your face again. Get the tabloids to talk about how you're back and replaced with an alien robot clone of you or something."

Atsushi walked out with Aoi's sunglasses, but Aoi didn't care. Okay, he cared a little bit, but not as much after hearing his voice sounded all right.

Aoi pulled out his phone and called Sato.

"He said it was good!" Aoi cheered after Sato picked up.

"I told you your voice sounded perfect," Sato replied.

"I know, but Atsushi was the first person who told me the truth. Even when I asked my agent, she said I sounded fine. I needed someone who worked with me before to really tell."

"As long as you feel confident now, that's all that matters to me."

Aoi plucked a piece of kimchi from the side dish and swallowed. "I should tell you, he made me take a photo with him before he would tell me what he thought."

"What an asshole."

"At first he wanted me to kiss him, but I told him no."

"You should've punched him like you did during Christmas."

Aoi laughed. "I think he learned his lesson, a little. He stuck some stupid emojis there. I don't want you to think something happened."

"Oh honey, I know you wouldn't do anything like that. I trust you. Him no, but you would kick his butt if he tried to do anything."

Aoi smoothed his hand along his pants, wishing he could have the conversation with Sato beside him. Better yet with Sato at home where they could hug and kiss and not have to worry about other people staring.

"This place is really good. We should check it out sometime," Aoi said.

"Order something you think I'd like, and we can have it for dinner. It'll be like I went out with you there."

"Can I have your mushrooms?"

"Sure." Sato's laugh made Aoi miss him more.

"Come home quick tonight. Those spreadsheets will still be there tomorrow."

MAY

S ATO WATCHED AS AOI scribbled down some notes next to the margins of his *Wild Skies* script. He put the pen back between his teeth and flipped to the next page of the manga open beside him.

"I think you've read that series more than I have now," Sato said.

Aoi pulled out the pen and stuck out his tongue. "Are you worried I'll be a better Gundam otaku than you?"

"That's impossible."

Aoi grinned and pushed the manga aside. "You want to bet? I've been rereading the script and this series nonstop since before my vocal surgery. There's no way anyone is going to say that I got this role because I was popular."

"You shouldn't read those fan forums."

"It's hard when they send me messages. The fujoshi are so much easier to please. I moan and they're happy, but your Gundam fans are crazy compared to them. They don't think I know enough about Gundam to act in one. I'm about to take a picture of one of your display cases to prove I'm a mech suit fan."

Sato snatched the manga and pushed it across the table. "You're letting them get to you."

Aoi's shoulders slumped. "I know."

"How many times have you read through the script and series?"

"Not that many."

"But a lot more than you usually do."

"*Wild Skies* is different."

Sato pushed up his glasses. "Is it really?"

"Of course. This is going to be so huge and not in some niche thing but everywhere."

"But weren't all of the other stories you acted in as important to you as you think *Wild Skies* is for other people?"

"I guess."

"It sounds like all this extra stressing is because you're listening to everyone else and not yourself. I know a part of you took this because it was something I was into—"

"It would be good for my career to diversify, and I didn't want to be put with Atsushi for the rest of my life. Even then, I wouldn't have taken it if I didn't enjoy it. Some of your Gundam enjoyment has worn off on me."

Sato smiled. "That's good to know."

"We're not having more Gundam series marathons though."

"Damn."

Aoi laughed, and Sato flipped through the script.

"You don't have to put more effort into this than what you want to do," Sato said. "Let's go out. You've done nothing but *Wild Skies* stuff since you had surgery."

"Where do you want to go?"

"I've missed hearing you practice moaning for one thing."

Aoi grinned. "It sounds like you want to stay in more than go out."

Sato grabbed one of the drama CDs that Aoi acted in from the stand between the other anime soundtracks and indie visual rock. Damn, Aoi really did buy each edition of every single from all the bands of someone he knew.

"This is what I mean," Sato said. "Let's go to karaoke. It'll be like old times."

Aoi smiled and embraced Sato. "I remember the first time we went to one together."

"You teased me so much back then."

"It was easy, but you tease me right back now." Aoi's finger trailed down Sato's shirt and stopped at his pants, his voice purring in his ear. "Are you sure you don't want to stay?"

Sato's cock sprang to life. Aoi could turn even the most mundane sentence into an erotic poem of lust. Still, they hadn't gone out in forever.

"Let's go before I change my mind," Sato said.

The bright sun beat down on Sato's face. The full humidity of summer hadn't hit yet, but Sato could've enjoyed something a little cooler. Trapped in the office all day meant his wardrobe was nothing but long-sleeved shirts. Aoi had the right idea with a black tank and ripped jeans that made him look like a street model for some up-and-coming alternative brand.

The karaoke club wasn't much of a walk. They got their microphones and headed into their room.

"Want to order something to eat?" Sato asked.

"I thought you were going to feed me."

Sato's cheeks grew hot, and Aoi laughed. "I knew I could still get you to blush."

"Abuse of power."

Aoi grabbed his microphone. "Food works though. We can actually sing until it comes, then play the drama CD."

Living in the middle of the anime district meant the karaoke club had every opening and ending theme song the two could desire. Aoi chose the first one, a happy-go-lucky theme to a show they'd both watched as kids. Sato even joined in at the chorus. Sato was surprised Aoi knew it considering his parents hadn't allowed him to watch TV.

When it was Sato's turn, he chose a Gundam song, of course, and Aoi hummed through the ending theme song. When the food arrived, they paused to eat as Aoi flipped through the song book.

"Look, they have Lilith songs," Aoi said.

Sato glanced over the page. "They have so many. Jin will be happy."

Aoi typed in the code for one of the songs, and Sato instantly recognized it as the one Aoi had recorded the chorus for. There was a very clear gasp of sex.

"You said you missed my moaning." The grin on Aoi's face was one he always had right before they had sex in a surprising place. They'd done some heavy petting in a karaoke club before, but this grin promised much more.

After Jin's initial singing, the song descended into nothing more than instruments over Aoi's moans. Sato tugged on

Aoi's shirt and planted a kiss on his lips. Aoi's moans lulled in Sato's throat like he'd fed off his desire.

"I have missed them," Sato said.

Aoi stood and grabbed the CD. "You chose this one?"

Sato shrugged. "I haven't heard it yet."

"It's not because you secretly fantasize about me being your secretary?"

Aoi put the CD into the player, and soon the voice of Aoi talked about his enjoyment for starting his first day on the job.

"Where's the manga?" Aoi asked.

"Oh, I forgot to bring it with me."

"We can't pretend to be fujoshi without the manga." Aoi sighed. "I guess that means we'll have to make our own images to go with it."

In one smooth motion, Aoi straddled Sato's hips and pulled him into a deep kiss. Sato always submitted to Aoi, opening up his mouth and letting him inside. The first of Aoi's voice-acted moans came through the speakers, and Aoi pulled away with a grin.

"You always make me moan better than that," Aoi whispered into Sato's ear before giving it a playful nip.

Sato grabbed Aoi's waist, clutching onto him for that extra bit of friction on his crotch. He was so close he could smell the yuzu-scented shampoo Aoi used.

"You want to do this here?" Sato asked.

"It's not like we haven't before." Aoi glanced down to Sato's bulge in his slacks. "And it looks like someone is already excited."

"Your moans always excite me."

"Prove it."

A wave of lust flooded over Sato. Aoi smashed his lips against his in a deep-rooted pleasure. Sato's glasses scratched his nose as their kiss deepened. Aoi purred into Sato's mouth as the room echoed with Aoi's recorded moans. Sato's toes curled, and he slid his hand underneath Aoi's tank and pressed against the warmth of his skin. Aoi rocked against Sato, their crotches touching. A wave of heat pulsed through his body.

Aoi pulled away from the kiss with a gasp. He grabbed Sato's glasses and put them on the table.

"I almost forgot how big you are." Aoi smiled and palmed Sato's hard-on through the fabric of his pants.

Aoi could say such dirty things without even the slightest hesitation. Sato had gotten better at writing the dirty things out during Aoi's vocal rest, but they caught in Sato's throat every time he tried to speak his lascivious thoughts.

"You're so wonderful," Sato whispered huskily.

It was far from what he thought. He wanted to say how the fact they were out in public brought him to a new edge. How a part of him wanted someone to come in so they could flaunt their relationship. He wanted everyone to know they belonged to each other. How Aoi still drove him wild each and every time, but it simply came out as "you're so wonderful." Sato could kick himself if he wasn't so turned on.

Aoi hooked a finger on the top of Sato's pants and popped the button free, then carefully grabbed hold of the zipper. Sato's hand covered Aoi's.

"I didn't bring any lube," Sato said.

Aoi drew down Sato's zipper and pulled out his cock. "Haven't you learned by now how naughty I am and that I always bring some with me when we go out?"

Sato's mouth opened, and he watched Aoi give his length a few determined strokes before sliding off his lap. He sprawled out on the sofa and pulled a small bottle of lube from his pocket. Had he planned the whole thing? There was always a bit of heavy petting when they listened to the drama CDs, but they never went all out before.

"Help me out of these," Aoi said, already undoing his own zipper.

Sato licked his lips and grabbed the waistband of Aoi's pants and underwear. He pulled them down while Aoi raised his hips. He was sheer perfection, his erect cock sticking straight in the air. He sat on the coffee table, legs out and open for Sato to see everything. Sato opened his mouth to take all of Aoi in.

"Let me ride you." Aoi's voice came out in a mix of desperation mixed with a dominant heat.

Sato could've cum right from just those words.

Aoi chuckled. "I'll take that as a yes."

Sato unclicked the lube and slathered it on his cock. Aoi held out his hand, and Sato gave him the half-empty bottle.

"Watch me," Aoi said. "It turns me on so much."

Sato didn't need to be asked twice, and each slow movement from Aoi was deliberate, from the little smirk on his face to the slow teasing outside his hole before sliding in one finger.

"Do you like watching too?" Aoi asked.

More teasing, but Sato didn't mind. He licked his lips, hoping to lubricate his thoughts. He could tell Aoi he was biggest turn-on in the world to him. How he imagined his cock heavy in his mouth or how he was already jealous of Aoi's fingers.

Yet as he stared at Aoi, his mouth open and his eyes closed, Sato could tell Aoi knew all the things he wanted to say.

Aoi opened his legs a little wider. "Are you watching?"

"Yeah."

"I can't wait for your cock to be in me." Aoi arched his back, tilted his head, and let out a sharp gasp followed by a slow string of hitched moans, each one coming out more lustfully than the next. No wonder he got paid to moan.

"What are you waiting for, then?" Sato somehow managed to get out.

Aoi slid his fingers out of him, letting out a small groan from the back of his throat at the loss. He stood in front of Sato, Aoi's long black tank covering his ass, but with his cock standing at attention, the fabric draped around it like an erotic work of art.

"How much do you want your cock in me?" Aoi asked.

Even bottoming, Aoi dominated.

"Aoi, please," Sato managed to say.

Aoi bent his knee on the sofa and trailed his hand down Sato's throat.

"Come on, you can do it. I remember all those dirty things you wrote down."

"Aoi…"

He ran his fingers through Sato's hair. "How you wanted me to pull at your hair as you sucked me dry."

Sato's nerves ignited. It was so much easier to write it down. It was like it wasn't really him wishing for the things that would usually make him blush to think.

"Tell me what you want?" Aoi suckled on the side of Sato's neck. "Come on, speak up. I know you have dirty thoughts swirling in your head."

"I want—I want…"

Aoi's placed his other knee on the sofa, hovering above Sato's cock. All of his thoughts collided, screaming for Aoi. He wanted him and only him for now. Forever.

"Want do you want me to do, Masatomo?"

Using his first name always cut through the maelstrom in Sato's mind.

"Ride me," he said.

"There we go. I knew you could do it."

A wave of heat flushed through Sato from the simple praise. Then Aoi grabbed the base of Sato's cock and guided himself down. Sato moaned, but it was nothing compared to the slurry Aoi let out. It was like hearing Aoi for the first time. His throat was finally free and able to stir the animalist desire with precisions from years of practice.

The characters in the drama CD were doing the same, yet the recorded gasps Aoi let out were muffled. They weren't the same as the quick moans and delightful purrs Aoi let out for Sato.

"You ready for this?" Aoi asked. "Because I'm ready for you to fill me up with your cum so much it leaks out."

"Yeah."

"Say my name every time I take you all the way in. You can do that, right? I know you can do it for me."

Sato could only nod. Aoi sank down, slow at first so Sato could easily keep up with Aoi's verbal demands through the ecstasy.

"Aoi," Sato moaned.

He rose, agonizingly slow, before moaning as he came back down, eating up all of Sato's dick.

"Say my name."

"Aoi."

Then his pace grew faster, and Sato calling out Aoi's name became a slur of incoherent moans between syllables.

"Louder. Make sure everyone can hear you!"

Sato met Aoi with each thrust, and with a few quick jerks of his hips, Sato came, with Aoi following shortly after.

Aoi wrapped his arms around Sato's neck and caught his breath.

"I love you," Aoi let out with a contented sigh.

Sato wrapped his arms around Aoi and squeezed. "I love you too."

JUNE

"I'M HOME," AOI SAID. "How was your day, Nightingale?"

Aoi walked over to the goldfish and grabbed the fish food shaker.

His mouth fell open.

Nightingale wasn't swimming around the tank or hiding in the little castle or even playing between the hot-pink plastic seaweed. Instead of any of the other things fish did, Nightingale floated on top of her tank.

"Shit." Aoi pressed his lips together. "But you did last longer than I thought you would."

Aoi and Sato had gone to a summer festival almost a year ago and won the fish. Aoi hadn't expected her to last more than a few days, but the weeks turned into more than a month.

Once she'd reached two months, Sato spent a weekend researching for the perfect upgrade to her bowl, only to learn they'd put her in danger by giving her a bowl in the first place. So they'd bought a good-sized tank and rearranged a section of manga and mech models to accommodate her new home size.

Aoi grabbed a cup and fished her out of her tank but then put her back. Nightingale belonged to both of them, so he couldn't dispose of her without Sato there. Aoi left Nightingale to her watery grave and prepared dinner. A nice curry rice with potatoes would be a little spice to the summer heat. It wouldn't feel as hot if they were eating something with a kick to it. Sato sometimes didn't understand the logic, but it always worked.

From cutting the potatoes to watching the swirling of steam rising from the rice cooker, Aoi loved every second of cooking. Sato had done so much for him, and taking the time each night to prepare their meal was Aoi's way of thanking him for everything.

Aoi leaned against the counter, the simmering pot of curry letting out the occasional bubble. There were a few months before the series would be released, but Aoi was excited for them to watch it together. His first series on national TV.

Recording *Wild Skies* had been different than the other voice acting gigs he'd done. Everyone else had recorded their parts while Aoi had recovered from surgery, so he got to play off the other actors and their parts. It challenged him not to relay on moaning the juicy bits, because there were none. His perfected moans of someone playing bottom meant nothing. He had to put all of his emotions through each line of dialogue.

"I'm home," Sato called.

Aoi bounced into the entry and planted a kiss on Sato's lips.

"You showed all the spreadsheets who was boss."

"A few of them. Some survived for tomorrow."

"You'll defeat them."

Sato sniffed the air. "What smells so good?"

"Curry rice."

They divided up the food and ate at the kotatsu. Aoi waited to see if Sato would notice their pet's demise, but no luck.

"I have some bad news," Aoi said.

Sato pushed up his glasses. "What?"

Aoi pointed to Nightingale. Sato followed his finger and frowned when he got to the fish.

"She made it a long time," Sato said.

"Almost a year."

Sato reached out and grabbed Aoi's hand. "You looked so handsome in that yukata the day we got her."

They were still having trouble with Sato's parents back then. It was amazing how they'd come around.

"Poor Nightingale," Sato said.

"I think she had a good life."

"Especially when you came home with that castle. She'd peek out of it when we'd feed her."

"Or how she'd follow your finger across the tank."

Aoi swallowed his last bit of curry. "She was a good fish."

"The best fish."

"Should we give her the funeral of all fish?"

"I guess."

Aoi dropped the dishes in the sink while Sato put Nightingale in a cup and began the funeral procession. Aoi followed him into the bathroom. They stood around the toilet.

"Do you want to say a few words?" Sato asked.

"I-ah…"

"She was a good fish, and may she live where all fishes go when it's their time."

Sato begin to turn the cup over, but then Aoi grabbed his wrist.

"Wait," Aoi said. "This doesn't feel right."

"What about it doesn't feel right?"

"Nightingale was such a good fish. I don't want to flush her down the toilet."

Sato raised an eyebrow. Aoi knew what he said was odd.

"You want to cremate her?" Sato asked.

"That's a bit much. But… the toilet?"

"You want to bury her?"

What was he thinking? But Nightingale was their pet. She was a living creature they'd both taken care of.

"I know it sounds silly."

"It's not silly. She was our goldfish, so if you want to bury her, I'm fine with that."

"That's what I want."

Sato found a small box, and Aoi pulled Nightingale from her cup, her fins sticking to herself and twisting against Aoi's skin. His eyes stung. He shouldn't have gotten so worked up.

"Do you want to go to the plot downstairs or the park?" Sato asked.

"The park. The one where we made the snow bunnies."

"Sounds like a good place."

They held hands down the hall of the apartment, only breaking the physical bond once they stepped outside. Businessmen gathered in the streets on their way to local bars, and students snuck in some quick shopping before heading to cram school.

Aoi and Sato found a quiet place in the park next to a bush. Aoi had brought a spoon to help dig the hole.

"She was a good fish," Aoi said. "She never tried to jump out of her tank, and she always ate her food."

Sato added. "She never got into trouble once."

They pushed the small mound of dirt over the box until it was completely covered. They waited there a few moments with Sato smiling up at Aoi. It felt odd to be making such a big deal over a tiny goldfish, but it was something they both cared for. They'd taken turns feeding, Sato doing it in the morning and Aoi in the afternoon. It was the death of something they shared.

"You ready?" Sato asked.

Aoi nodded and stood, brushing his jeans off.

"Yeah, let's head home."

They walked out of the park and back toward home.

"I was thinking," Aoi said. "What are we going to do with all of Nightingale's old stuff?"

Sato shrugged. "Throw it away, I guess."

"Let's get another goldfish to honor her memory."

"Really?"

"We can call her Nightingale the Second."

Sato smiled. "That sounds like a good idea."

"I thought so."

JULY

T HE SUSHI CHUGGED ALONG the conveyer belt while Aoi and Sato both picked up a plate of tuna nigiri.

"I can't believe it's already so late," Aoi said.

"The next place should have the right size for sure."

Aoi shot Sato a side eye and dipped his fish into a saucer of soy sauce. "You said that about the last two."

"The reviews said they had a range of sizes. They were the top ranked on my spreadsheet of rental stores."

"I'm starting to think you've lost your spreadsheet skills."

Sato gasped. "What a horrible thing to say."

"You gotta step it up if you want to maintain your crown as King of Spreadsheets."

Sato had spent most of the week researching the perfect tux rental shops in Tokyo, ranking them from star status with reviews to distance from home. His accountant brain somehow pieced together the best one, balancing the two to produce the master list of the best shops in Tokyo. So far everything had been a dud.

Sato shrugged. "Who knew tux shopping would be so hard?"

"It's because you're a giant." Aoi pointed to a cucumber roll that slipped passed him, and Sato snatched it before it could escape down the belt. He set it down between them.

"Maybe renting isn't the best idea." Sato plucked one of the rolls from the cluster.

"But it's so expensive to get one custom made. It's not like Jiro and Chie are getting married tomorrow. We still have a month to look for good rentals."

"The spreadsheet though. We're already to the middle selections. From here it's downhill."

"Oh yes, the spreadsheet knows all." Aoi laughed and shoved the empty plate down the slot.

Their plate counter went up, and a video of the ninja mascot of the restaurant played a short clip in front of them. The ninja defeated a monstrous octopus as big as a building. Then looming music played as a new threat of a snake slithered onto the screen. Oh no! It was another monster ready to destroy the city. The only way the ninja could save Tokyo was by eating more sushi.

An upbeat melody played, and a ball from the collection of capsule toys on top of the screen released. The red-and-white ball slid down the tube and popped out in front of them.

Sato grabbed it and cracked it open. "The expense wouldn't be so bad if I went to multiple weddings. Michiko's probably never tying the knot, so unless Jin and Kazuki do, then it would be a onetime thing."

"Maybe you should hang out with more people at work."

"All the wedding gift money would probably zap all the savings made up with the price per wear."

Aoi pointed to the plastic ball. "What did we get?"

A grin spread across Sato's face. He unpeeled the sticker of Pikachu and stuck on it Aoi's shirt. "Aoi, I choose you."

"You did not just summon me."

Sato's laughter grew louder until Aoi joined. If it wasn't for the suit frustration, it probably wouldn't be half as funny.

"If I go into a suit shop with this sticker on my shirt, everyone's going to think I'm five."

Sato snickered more, covering his mouth, but it only made him laugh harder.

"I know what you're thinking. Don't say it," Aoi warned.

"What? That it'll be more your height and not the sticker that would make people think you're five?"

"Let's get that sweet ass of yours into some bad-fitting clothes. You're getting too cocky."

Even the way Sato pushed up his glasses was a mix of sass and sexy. He'd learned to hit all of Aoi's turn-ons as well as he could create a spreadsheet formula.

They paid, and on the way out, Aoi handed the sticker to a little kid in the booth next to them.

The next rental shop was on the fifth floor of a building. It hid in a corner with a small paper sign. The name of the shop was above a picture of an anime girl. Aoi took a step back and raised an eyebrow.

"Trust the spreadsheet," Sato said.

"We don't accidentally want to get someone's cosplay the day of the wedding."

"Jiro probably wouldn't mind."

"But Chie would."

They stepped inside the small shop, getting an enthusiastic greeting from the middle-aged owner. His hair grayed in streaks but more heavily on his right side, reminding Aoi of an indie rocker he once knew.

At the first few stops they'd tried on suits at the same time, but after the third time, Aoi decided it worked better if Sato tried them on first. The stores could always make Aoi's tuxes work, but never his.

Sato explained what they were looking for to the owner. He took a few measurements and disappeared in a back room, leaving Sato to undress behind a curtain.

Aoi sat back in a worn leather chair. Duct tape covered one of the holes while white stuffing came out of a hole in the top.

"I don't think I can stand any more changing," Sato said from behind the curtain.

"We've been to five places."

"I think I might cave."

"Cave?"

"If they can't find me a rental, maybe it's better to get a tux tailor made."

"But the cost? Think of all the mech models you could buy."

Sato stuck his head out from behind the curtain and dramatically pushed up his glasses. "If only Jiro knew how I suffered for our friendship."

The owner came out and handed Sato a tux. Aoi waited, his leg jiggling. A stack of bridal magazines sat beside them, creating their own end table by sheer number. Surprisingly, they were all recent editions.

He grabbed one and scanned through the articles. Advertising lined most of the pages. Weddings could get so expensive for no reason. That was probably why everyone gave the couple money—so they could pay off the debt from the celebration.

Sato mumbled something under his breath, and Aoi flipped through a few more pages.

He stopped.

A spread of wedding bands took up a full page. Diamonds studded most of the bands, but in the corner sat two simple silver bands with a brushed finish. The lines next to it read that they were from the LGBT wedding ring collection. They were reasonably priced on top of it.

Aoi tilted his head. His heart thumped one slow beat after the next, ringing out his desire. The rings didn't look specially like wedding bands. It would be easy for Sato to wear to work and not draw unnecessary attention. Aoi sighed and turned the page. It wasn't like they could really get married anyway.

"Ready?" Sato said.

Aoi dropped the magazine. "Let's see."

Sato emerged. The pants nearly fell off his hips to get the length right, and the shirtsleeves stopped well above his wrist.

"This might be tough as a rental," the owner said.

Aoi shook his head. "How are you able to find your suits for work?

Sato shrugged. "I wear really long socks and hope no one notices. I sit behind a desk all day, so it usually doesn't draw attention."

The owner tried not to laugh. "We'll have to do a lot of tacking to get the pants right. Maybe size up the shirt too."

Sato sighed. "How much is it to get one tailored?"

The owner said the amount, and Sato turned to Aoi. "What do you think?"

Sitting at a boring wedding wasn't his best idea of spending a Saturday, but if Aoi could get a better view of Sato's ass, it would make the evening a little more interesting. It wasn't like Aoi could say that out loud, at least not while the owner stood there.

Aoi shrugged. "It's your Gundam collection."

"Are you attending the wedding too?" the owner asked.

"Yes, it's our mutual friend." It wasn't like Aoi could say they lived together as lovers so of course they'd both be invited to the wedding.

"If you both get a tailored tux, I'll offer you both a nice discount. You could reuse them for when you get married."

Sato turned around, catching himself in the mirror, and Aoi couldn't think of a worse way to spend a wedding with the saggy pants Sato would wear. Aoi would have to pass on his boy love manga for a bit, but he could always borrow the newest releases from Michiko.

"Only if you can make me look good enough to bring someone home that night." Aoi winked at Sato.

AUGUST

SATO ADJUSTED JIRO'S TIE. It would be the fifth time in the past fifteen minutes. The other groomsmen took turns refilling each other's champagne glasses, leaving Sato to his best-man duties.

"What happens if when I get there, she's not there?" Jiro asked.

"That's the point. She comes in after you."

"What if the music plays and she doesn't walk down the aisle?"

"I'm sure they won't play the music until they know she's there."

"True."

"See? Nothing to worry about."

Jiro smiled, but the lines around his eyes didn't disappear. He tugged at his tie and paced back down the length of the room. The other groomsmen brought Sato and Jiro their glasses of champagne. Jiro downed his so fast, Sato hadn't even had time to take his first sip. Sato had never seen Jiro stay quiet for so long. No matter what reassurance he gave, it was short-lived. The night before, he'd called Sato every few hours for encouragement.

The photographer came in and snapped a few photos of them all together. Then the wedding planner came in and sounded the five-minute start time. Jiro shook his hands and took in some deep breaths.

Sato squeezed his shoulder. "Don't worry, it'll be fine."

"I think I'm going to throw up."

"You don't want to mess up your tux, do you?"

Jiro pressed one hand against the wall and the other on his stomach.

"Take some deep breaths."

Jiro crumpled.

"Think of what made you want to propose to Chie in the first place. Then you'll be able to relax again."

"She was the one who proposed."

"Oh. Then what made you say yes? Was there a memory or time that made you think yes, she's the one?"

Jiro's fingers curled along the wall, and a smile crossed his face that warmed Sato. Jiro stood a little straighter and readjusted his tie.

"We went out to dinner and a movie when we first dated," Jiro said. "It was such an amazing night. We bought ice cream, and then I got on a huge tangent of about how I once had ice cream in this place in Osaka. I know I can drag things on and on. When I realized how much I dragged on and on, I looked at her and realized she'd paid attention to the whole thing. So many people start to ignore me, but she was there. That's when I thought we'd work."

"Go there, then, when you're waiting for Chie to go down the aisle. She's probably thinking of her own happy memory of you right now."

The wedding planner called for the start, and Jiro walked down the red-carpeted aisle with Sato following behind.

Sato slipped his hands into his pocket for a quick check to see if the rings were still there. All the points he'd gotten for being a good best man would've been lost if they weren't. He touched them then and pulled his hands out and positioned them the way the photographer said to do during the rehearsal. He let out a peaceful sigh and glanced over the flowers decorating the venue.

His thoughts drifted once he couldn't spot Aoi amongst the crowd. He remembered the first moment he'd decided Aoi was the person he wanted to spend the rest of his life with.

Aoi had practiced for months to run in a marathon during the humid summer. He'd trained for so long Sato had even run with him a few times. Well, maybe not with him, but he kept up for a few minutes, then Aoi would jump ahead. When the day came, Sato waited along the path, and even his parents had come along to cheer. At the time, their relationship had been on rocky ground.

When Aoi had passed by, he was well behind the pack of leaders, but even then he'd kept on pushing. He ran for the enjoyment of it. When he'd seen Sato, he gave him a high five. He held on a second longer and gave a big squeeze before breaking away. Anyone could have seen. Then Aoi's hand had slipped free, and with it he took Sato's heart.

The music played, and the flower girl came down, dropping a few rose petals before completely ignoring it to run toward her mother at the front seat. The room chuckled and then stood as the doors reopened and Chie entered.

Sato caught a glimpse of Aoi. The custom blue suit hugged his runner's body, and the sprig of pink flowers on his lapel matched his bubbly personality. He wasn't looking at Chie but at him. The smile on his face was like the one on the day he'd won the race at his own pace. Sato would probably feel like Jiro when they'd get married. He'd worry and drink too much and then be the happiest man on Earth seeing Aoi walk down the aisle.

Would Aoi walk down to meet him? Maybe Sato would be the one walking? How were those things decided? It wasn't like one of them would be wearing a dress. They could walk down together. Everyone they knew would be there and… His thoughts flooded out in breathless heaves of melancholy, tainted more and more with bitterness.

Chie and Jiro could get their love validated and celebrate with everyone, and no one would think any different. While for Sato to visit Aoi in a hospital, he had to fill out a million different forms and still could've been rejected if the staff felt like it. He'd never be able to marry Aoi with how slow the government handed out equal rights. Sure, there were a few prefectures allowing it, but unless the whole country did, the certificate wouldn't mean the same to everyone.

"Sato," Jiro said. "The rings."

He handed them over but then snapped his attention back to Aoi. The same smile was on his face, but there was a dull sadness in his eyes. It would be nice when the whole thing was over. Maybe with the Olympic games happening in Japan, it would put some international pressure on Japan to hurry up and get with the rest of the modern world.

Still, as the ceremony drew to its end, Aoi never looking anywhere else but at Sato, he reminded himself that one day he'd be able to introduce him as his husband.

SEPTEMBER

AOI RUBBED HIS HANDS against a frayed, stylized rip on his jeans. His costar on *Wild Skies*, Kaya, sat in the makeup chair beside him. The interview today was his last before the premier later tonight. Aoi's stomach flopped like a decaying Gundam knocked over by the wind.

"Close your eyes for me." Aoi's makeup woman dabbed her brush into some powder.

"Are you excited?" Kaya asked.

"Of course! It's nice they're interviewing us together. When I'm by myself, it's not as fun."

"It's nice to finally work with you in person. I met the other voice actors before, but not you, since you were recovering when we recorded."

Aoi smiled. "Your wonderful voice acting gave me so much to work with when I was recording."

She laughed, pushing black hair over her shoulder. "No need for compliments. We're not on camera yet."

The makeup artist gave them both a final dose of powder and sent them on their way backstage.

Kaya pulled out her phone. "Do you know how to get the special ending?"

Aoi glanced at the screen, where the intro of *Nephilim Boys' School* was playing. It was a dating sim Aoi had made last year.

"The special ending?" Aoi asked.

"Where you get with all the guys."

Aoi laughed. "I have no idea. I haven't even played it."

She frowned, tapping away at some of the prompts. "It's so addicting. I picked it up when I heard you were doing the recording and still do the daily check-in. You and Atsushi work so well together."

Aoi bit the inside of his cheek. "He's got a good voice."

"That's for sure." She tapped her phone for a second. "You really have no idea?"

"There's probably a walk-through online."

She closed the app. "That's cheating."

"But asking me isn't?"

"No, because you're one of the characters."

"Right."

"What? It totally doesn't count as cheating."

"As long as you tell yourself that."

The show began. They pulled Aoi and Kaya onto the set and chatted with them for a few minutes about them and the show.

Aoi's whole body buzzed. Never before had there been so much fanfare for something he'd acted in. In less than twelve hours, the show everyone had been talking about for months would premiere. He'd sit back and watch everyone in Japan talk and form some kind of opinion.

"Aoi, it's nice to see you back," the host said. "You had some health issues."

He rubbed the back of his neck. "Yes, I am all better now. Thanks, everyone, for your support while I was away. I'm excited to be back."

The audience cheered.

The host asked some questions to Kaya, and Aoi could only half pay attention. His thoughts carried him away to Sato. Aoi had planned their evening together. After the interview, he'd go home and cook Sato's favorite meal. They'd watch the show together. The ending would play and then the preview would end, and when Sato opened his mouth to say what he thought of the series, then Aoi would ask him the question he'd wanted to for months.

"We have a lot of good wishes from people in the audience we wanted to show you both," the host said.

There was a small screen off to the side playing the video clips of the audience saying how excited they were for the upcoming show. Then the setting changed to an older woman and man. They congratulated Kaya and said how proud they were of her. The smile on her face couldn't be bigger.

"Who were they?" the host asked.

"They're my parents."

"We have a special message for you too, Aoi."

Aoi's raised an eyebrow. Sato? No. It couldn't be him. Sato wouldn't come all the way out on national TV. He worked in accounting, so it would put his job at too much risk. Maybe Sato's parents. That would be sweet of them, or Jin. It had to be Jin. They wouldn't turn down the opportunity to bring a famous rock star onto the show. Maybe lumping them together would put Lilith on the right track for Tokyo Dome status.

The host turned to Aoi. "You like to cook."

"It's fun to make things that others can enjoy."

"From what I hear, you learned to cook at an early age."

No. It was impossible.

"You helped out at your family's restaurant."

The video played, and the same host was in the footage. He strolled the all-too-familiar street, giving exposition that barely registered with Aoi.

His parents popped on the screen, going over the different dishes at the restaurant inspired by Aoi. His favorite appetizer. His favorite style of ramen. They named them after him and characters he acted. They were using his name to sell food.

"Do you have any words you want to say to him?" the host asked Aoi's parents in the video.

His mom smiled. She actually smiled. "I'm excited to see how the new series comes out."

"We hope the show is a big success," his dad added.

Aoi's mouth dropped, his throat dried, and fire burned in his veins. The people who'd kicked him out when he was a teen, who'd told him they didn't have a son, used his name to sell food. Even then, during all the clips, they never apologized or hinted at any remorse for what they did. They smiled for the show. They smiled for hope of bringing more of his fans to their restaurant to fork over their money. They didn't give a fuck about him.

"I can't believe it," Aoi said. "I haven't seen them in a long time."

The host reminded everyone to watch the show later that night. The show wrapped, and Aoi walked off set. He ran to the backstage bathroom and banged his fist against the door.

He winced, pain shooting down his knuckles to his elbow. He slid down the wall and buried his head on his knees. He could've dissolved into a puddle of urine on the floor if he hadn't been so fucking angry. Every emotion cooked inside him until hot tears ran down his cheeks.

His parents had never tried to contact him to apologize. He'd read every one of his fan letters and never once stumbled across one sent from his parents. They couldn't get away with taking money from his fans. He'd finally tell them to their faces everything they deserved, and it had to be before tonight.

SEPTEMBER BONUS

HOW MANY TIMES HAD Sato walked by the jewelry store without a second thought? Hundreds? Thousands? But for the past month, he'd noticed it more and more. He'd slow down, sneaking in a quick glance. The next week, the glances lengthened until he'd stop and take in the display, his attention fixating on the men's wedding bands.

Today when he stared at the display, his heart fluttered, ready to leap out of his throat and fly across the city to Aoi's side. He swallowed, but he couldn't keep his fluttering desire down another day. Today was the day. Sato knew from his heart to his bones to every neuron in his brain. He and Aoi had swirled around the idea for months, but it would finally happen today. He'd ask Aoi to marry him.

Jiro had mentioned seeing wedding bands for gay couples when he and Chie bought theirs. Sure, he could've gotten two men's-style rings from any collection, but getting a pair especially made for gay couple made Sato feel normal when everything else about a gay wedding would be considered abnormal to the government.

Sato opened the door. Everything about the store spar-kled, and the bright lights made it all flash. Classical music played, and the store employees greeted him. One asked if he needed help with anything, but Sato froze and said it was fine.

Maybe it would be easier if he bought the rings online. He pressed his lips together. Sure, that might be a better idea if he had three days to plan and a week to get them shipped. Aoi's premiere would be in less than five hours. Another day too long for his fluttering heart to wait.

"Are you looking for a particular style, sir?" the sales assistant asked.

"Yeah, let's see." Sato pushed up his glasses, keeping his hand up to cover his burning face. Maybe he'd have more courage if he wrote it down. He pointed to the cluster of rings. "This style."

"Of course, sir. If you'd like, I can take these rings to one of our private viewing areas." His voice hadn't changed; in fact, when Sato dropped his hand, the assistant smiled like he was any other customer.

"Out here is fine."

Sato doubted anyone would really take notice. Still, it was a nice gesture and cooled Sato's burning face.

The assistant pulled out the display from the locked case. The selection wasn't huge, but it was probably for the best. If there had been any more, he'd want to analyze them and create a spreadsheet ranking of each.

Sato skipped the flashier selections with diamonds across the band. Sato wanted matching rings, and something so flashy wouldn't appeal to Aoi, especially the price. The silver ones with a brush finish would be perfect. The brushed part had a rocker edge to it that Aoi would enjoy, but it still looked classic enough Sato could wear it to work without drawing unnecessary attention.

"Can I try this one?" Sato asked.

"Absolutely. Let's take your ring size."

It took a few seconds of the assistant using his coil of rings to find Sato's size. He slipped the ring on his hand, holding it out and then pulling it close. He closed his eyes, imagining it on Aoi's finger and how their hands would look with their fingers laced with the bands on. Everyone could finally see the love they had for each other with just a glance.

"I'll take two of these," Sato said.

"Do you know the other ring size?"

The wings of Sato's heart burned away, flightless, and plummeted into his stomach. He didn't know Aoi's ring size.

"Don't worry, it happens all the time. We'll take a guess, and if it's wrong, you can get it exchanged at no charge for up to two weeks."

"Good. I planned on asking tonight, so if it doesn't fit, you'll see me here tomorrow." Sato chuckled. "I think his fingers are thinner than mine, so maybe a few sizes down."

It took only a few more minutes for Sato to pay and get a box for the rings.

All during the train ride home, he imagined how the evening would play out. He'd come home to a nice warm meal from Aoi. Sato had suggested they'd go out to celebrate the premiere, but Aoi said he'd cook a better meal at home for much cheaper. They'd eat and snuggle while watching the premiere. The ending credits would play and then the preview for next week. Sato would get on one knee and say…

Shit, what was he going to say? He'd spent so much time thinking about rings and the right time to ask, but what was he going to say when he proposed?

Sato bit his lip, stepping off the train at his stop. Maybe the words would come to him when he was in the moment. No. He had a hard enough time answering Aoi's questions when they screwed, and most of those were easy "put it in" kinds of things. He'd take a bath before dinner and spend some time scribbling out something.

They'd lived together for so long. When Aoi went in for his surgery, they'd tied their financial and legal lives together. They were already basically married. If they waited for all of Japan to accept their love, they could both be dead before it happened. Sato wanted the marriage for them, not for anyone else, to deepen their bond.

"I'm home," Sato called, opening the door.

Aoi mumbled a reply, and Sato frowned. Something wasn't right. The house didn't smell of delicious food, and Aoi didn't sound like an actor about to be in the anime of the next decade.

Sato walked deeper into the apartment to Aoi. His backpack lay open like a hungry mouth. His nostrils flared, and his chest thrusted out.

"What's going on?" Sato asked.

"I'm packing."

"I can see that. Why are you packing?"

Aoi shoved a handful of clothes inside and jerked the zipper up. "Because my parents are assholes, and I'm finally going to tell it to their faces."

"But the premiere is tonight."

"And they'll make a shit ton of money if I don't confront them now."

Aoi turned, making his way to the bathroom, but Sato took his arm. "Tell me what's going on?"

Aoi's curt laugh sent a chill down Sato's spine. Aoi explained everything about his parents using his name to sell food without even offering up an apology. He broke out of Sato's hold and grabbed the toothpaste.

"I'm going to stay there for as long as it takes. It's not right."

"Okay, I get it. Let me get my bag."

"No."

"You don't have to face them alone."

Sure, proposing at a hotel wasn't exactly what Sato had in mind, but it would work. He could give some half-formed speech trying to express his deeper feelings anywhere.

"You don't need to get involved with their shit," Aoi said.

"We're a couple. We handle things together."

"You don't understand. They're not like your parents. Yours tried to understand; mine kicked me out without a second thought."

"All the more reason for us to do it together."

Aoi pushed his bag onto his shoulder. "If you come, it would make it worse. I need to handle them by myself."

Sato's body tensed at the words. "Why can't you trust me to help?"

"It's not you." Aoi squeezed Sato's hand. "It's them. They're out of my life. Have been for a long time now. I don't want you to know them. You're so perfect, Sato. They don't deserve to meet you."

Sato pulled Aoi close and wrapped his arms around him. "You call me anytime and I'll answer, okay?"

"I will. Hopefully it won't take more than a day or two to clean up this mess."

"Good."

Sato bent down and kissed Aoi, trying to put everything into it, all the emotions ringing in his heart, but Aoi pulled away much too quickly.

"Love you," Aoi whispered.

"You too."

The door shut behind Aoi, and Sato sighed. The rings in his pocket weighed him down like a heavy stone. He pulled the velvet box out and set it next to their new goldfish.

"It's us, Nightingale II."

AOI'S BONES ACHED from his rage. His pent-up energy through the train ride and bus stop cut into his very marrow, leaving him as bitter as the days he couldn't find anywhere to sleep. The streets had been cold, and he'd pushed all his hatred and sadness into a ball. He'd pass that ball of fury to his parents and never think about it again. He had his new life with Sato to worry about, and with one big sweep he could bury every last part of his past behind him.

The TV show thankfully never showed the front of his parents' restaurant, which was good, because Aoi was convinced he would've died on set if he'd seen it. Most of the outside resembled what it had for years, dark brown wood with a sign reading "Hirayama's" at the top, but next to the sign stood a stylized mini character of him mounted to the top. Outside seating was added no doubt to deal with influx of customers.

He ground his teeth together and drew closer. A paper sign on the door encouraged people to come and dine at the restaurant Aoi had grown up in. Aoi rolled his eyes and clutched the door handle.

He opened the door. The same smell: old wood and a seeping of soy sauce. The display cases were the same, but now the same cartoon version of him from the outside was making recommendations with speech bubbles—"taste yummy" or "careful, spicy." Covers of the drama CDs hung on the wall. Even the menu had a cartoon version of him winking at the best dishes.

The same sign printed on the outside saying how Aoi grew up here was also repeated on the display case, along with several of Aoi's favorite food items. He wanted to vomit. He grabbed the edge and ripped the paper off. Aoi wouldn't be surprised if they didn't have everyone dress up like him during dinner.

"Excuse me, sir. You can't—"

"I want to see the Hirayamas."

The hostess left, and the manager came over. No surprise since he'd caused such a scene. If only it hadn't been the time between lunch and dinner, then he could show more people the true nature of his parents' praise of their child's talent.

"Who are you?" he asked. "Do you have an appointment with them?"

Aoi pointed at the cardboard cutout cartoon version of him beside the hostess stand. "I'm him."

He glanced to the cutout and then back at Aoi and crossed his arms.

"I want to speak to my parents." Aoi's voice stayed firm even if his insides trembled with rage.

"You need to make an appointment."

Aoi grabbed the strap of his backpack so hard he thought he'd tear it out. Everyone at the restaurant blocked his path. Whatever. He didn't need their permission. He'd knew his father would be in his little office next to the employee restroom. His mother would be tucked in the nook behind his father, going over the books or prepping in the kitchen if they'd fallen behind.

He ignored what the manager said and walked right past him. He kept on calling behind, but Aoi wouldn't be deterred.

He slammed open the office door. It hung against the desk his parents shared.

"How fucking dare you!" Aoi screamed.

"What are you doing here?" Mother asked.

"I'm already all over the walls. I might as well be here in the flesh. Maybe you can take a picture of me in every booth and sell those to the highest bidder."

"Get a hold of yourself."

"It's wrong to use my name when you l-left me home-less." Aoi's voice cracked. The little ball of hatred exploded inside of him. He slammed his fist against the door. "How could you?"

His father's glare pushed Aoi back twenty years, like he'd thrown a tantrum because he couldn't watch TV like the other kids. Father's reading glasses sank low on his nose. His finger hadn't moved from the line on the computer screen.

"If it wasn't for how we treated you, you wouldn't be half as successful as you are now," he said.

"You? I was the one who did all the work. I was the one who struggled. You did nothing for me. You only made it worse. You kicked me out without even telling me why. You pretended I was dead for years until you realized you could profit off my face."

"Get out of here," his mom's haggard voice cracked in.

She did what she always did and butted in between arguments and sent Aoi to his room. Then she'd find some possession of his to take and throw in the trash, forcing him to watch while Dad lectured some more. Why did he feel like a powerless child again? The manager came and apologized for the intrusion, trying to shut the door with Aoi wedged between it.

"You're making money off my name!" Aoi yelled, pushing back against the door. "You have me to thank for all these profits. I made a name for myself. I found a man who loves me for me. Something you could never understand."

"Call the police," Mom said.

Dad stood from behind the desk, his glasses never leaving his face, like even talking to his son he hadn't seen in years wasn't worth the effort of looking up from his paperwork. Aoi's heart quivered, and doubt flooded his thoughts.

"All you ever did was use people. You used us, living in our house and knowingly not following our rules or that of decent society. You're probably using whoever you're with now. You always took whatever you wanted and never gave anything back. We're finally getting back all those years we had to put up with you. Get out. You're not welcome."

Aoi's legs wobbled like soba noodles. He didn't want to run. He wanted to stand up and show his parents the pain they put him through. But in less than five minutes, they stripped him down and tore into all his strength.

He obeyed, leaving the restaurant and all hopes of righting the wrong.

PEOPLE PACKED THE Mechanics Lounge bar like a train during rush hour. One of the other anime-themed bars wouldn't have had such a crowd, but where else would Sato go for the premiere of the biggest Gundam anime of the decade? The audio echoed in the bar, so even with people mumbling, everyone could hear the show. They all cheered as the opening theme played.

Sato and Jiro had come early enough to grab one of the last tables cramped in a corner.

"I'll have another," Sato told the bartender.

"You're really partying," Jiro said.

Sato pushed up his glasses and took a gulp from his glass. What else was he supposed to do on the day he had planned to propose to his boyfriend, who'd left him to deal with family drama?

"Thanks for joining me," Sato said. "I couldn't watch this alone."

"Aoi didn't want to watch it with you?"

Sato rubbed his forehead. "He had a family emergency."

"Oh, too bad. I'll tell you, Chie's glad she didn't have to watch it with me. So I'm happy you called me up for a beer and to watch it here. I feel like a bachelor all over again." Jiro laughed.

The opening song faded, and Aoi's character, Hiro, appeared onscreen as a child, staring up at a big mech suit from his space station window. When he spoke, Sato's heart clutched. His body grew numb, and the air pushed out of his lungs like he'd been punched.

He knew he'd had to leave the apartment or else he'd spend the night moping—or, worse, crying his eyes out with only their goldfish for company. He'd thought the excitement of everyone else would lift his sprits. He was wrong.

"Aoi sounds really good," Jiro said.

"He's amazing."

"But like, if I closed my eyes and thought about what Hiro would sound like, it would be him. He might even be better than I imagined. He's got the plucky sound but one that's determined when push comes to shove."

"He must've read the manga and scripts over a dozen times to get the voice right."

They watched the show for a bit. Everyone at the lounge enjoyed Aoi's voice acting. It cut to a commercial break, and a flood of men dove into the restrooms. Jiro laughed.

"When does Aoi get back?" he asked. "Then I know when you'll stop moping around."

"I'm not moping," Sato lied.

"What's supposed to be the best Gundam series is currently on air and you've been acting like someone insulted you."

Sato rubbed his thumb along the outside of his glass. Aoi's parents had insulted their son, so it was like they insulted him.

"Aoi's parents are assholes. They had a huge falling out ages ago, but now they've been using his name to sell more food." Sato raked his fingers through his hair, leaving it in every direction. "He wanted to deal with it himself. I get it, sure, but I don't know how long this is going to take."

Jiro slid his beer back and forth. "That is a tough one."

"I wish I could help some way. I texted him before I left to see if he was okay, but he hasn't replied." Sato took in a deep breath. "I was hoping to propose to him after the show was over."

"Really? Congratulations!"

"Don't." Sato banged his forehead against the table. "Aoi left, and I barely got an explanation. I had it all planned out, and then poof. All because of his parents. They ruined what was going to be one of *my* happiest days too."

"Isn't there something his agent can do?"

"What do you mean?"

"Aoi's been in the news and media a lot with the series and when he came out. Would he be considered a public figure now? So using his name without permission would be illegal, wouldn't it?"

"You're right!"

Wings exploded out of Sato's heart, and he could've soared his way to Aoi's side.

AOI COULDN'T EVEN turn on the TV in his hotel room. Though he doubted it would have the premium channel for *Wild Skies*. Aoi had selected it because it was the cheapest one close to the restaurant.

He sighed and plopped on the bed. His hair was damp after his shower. The water had gone cold with how long he'd spent under the shower, washing away his tears. He really was that predictable.

He curled into a ball and traced the honeybees on the thin hotel bedding a few times before grabbing his backpack and fishing out the velvet box holding Sato's ring. Aoi had taken it so Sato wouldn't accidently find it.

Aoi opened the box, then closed it, then opened and closed it again. He stared at the wedding band. It had to be the stupidest idea he'd ever had. Only a few prefectures recognized gay marriage. Those really didn't mean anything until the courts finally ruled it legal.

He slammed the box shut and stretched out.

His parents were right. Sato had supported most of Aoi for the whole year while his voice was jacked up. He'd taken his support with everything, even used it to finally get the surgery done. He'd used Sato.

Aoi was stupid for wanting to propose. He'd been trouble for Sato from the start. That was why Sato had only bothered to text once. He really didn't care that he was gone.

THE STAINED CEILING of the cheap hotel resembled a bunny jumping over a hedge. Aoi remembered reading a script about a Shinto priest onmyoji who'd said stains on ceilings were created by a monster yokai licking the spot. It would be his luck picking a hotel filled with monsters. Made sense since happy people wouldn't choose a hotel that advertised color TV as a luxury feature. If only he could say a few magical words and fix everything.

He turned and buried his head in his pillow and drew the thin blankets over him. He didn't want to leave until he exterminated every cartoonish picture and mention of him from the restaurant. But he was powerless against his parents. He'd tried and failed, like he had in every situation growing up.

Maybe he should go back home. He'd still be miserable, but Sato would be there. He'd figure out some way to lift his spirits. He was too good for him.

Aoi's phone vibrated. A text. Probably Sato seeing if he was okay, or his agent.

He groaned, stretching for his phone on the nightstand, but it was too far. Whatever. Was it even worth trying to go back to the restaurant today for his parents to beat him down again?

His phone rang. He rolled over to grab it. It was Sato. Aoi sighed and answered.

"You're still close to your parents' place?" Sato asked.

"Why?"

"I'm going to be at their restaurant in ten minutes."

Aoi sighed. "Don't bother. They're still assholes."

"Well, I'm meeting you there, so hurry up. You'll want to see this."

Sato hung up before Aoi could protest.

He dressed, shoving the ring in his jeans pocket so nothing would happen to it. He walked the short distance to the restaurant. A line of people waited outside with lunchtime in full swing. Aoi slid on his sunglasses and hoped no one would recognize him. The last thing he needed was to create some kind of scene with a million fans close by.

Sato stood a distance away dressed in the suit he always wore when he attended a meeting with his boss. His freshly polished shoes, slicked-back hair, and briefcase made him look like the hot new accountant at some company topping the Tosho Exchange. If the situation had been different, Aoi would've felt a stirring of desire ring through him with just a glance, but not with all the crap that was going on.

"What's going on?" Aoi asked. "And why do you look like you have a team of people working under you?"

Sato pushed up his glasses, his eyes narrowing. "Where are they?"

"What are you doing?"

"Are they in the back?"

"It's the middle of the lunch rush."

"Good. The more people the better with this. Come on, we're ending this now."

Sato sprang ahead, keeping a brisk pace Aoi had never seen on their walks together. He bypassed the line waiting to get inside and stopped at the host station.

"I need to speak with Mr. and Mrs. Hirayama, the owners of this establishment." Sato's voice came out lower than Aoi usually heard.

The hostess blinked a few times, her mouth agape.

"Now," Sato added. "This is a very important legal matter."

She disappeared into the back, and Aoi tugged on Sato's arm.

"What do you think you're doing?"

"You'll see. This is what is best for us."

A few of the ladies waiting in line looked at the cardboard cutout and then back at Aoi, while a few already at their tables whipped out their cell phones. Aoi bit the inside of his cheek, hoping the pain would distract him from his panic.

His parents actually came out, no doubt thinking they could make Aoi's defeat a public matter. They probably wanted everyone to see how ungrateful their son was.

"I'm Mr. Hirayama's lawyer." Sato propped his briefcase on the hostess stand and pulled out a paper. "We tried to handle this matter quickly, and you did not accept. So I'm here to issue this official cease-and-desist letter. You needed Mr. Hirayama's explicit permission to use his name in a commercial context. You have thirty days to take all refer-ences down, or we will bring this to court."

Sato thrust the paper into their hands. Their mouths dropped, and for the first time in Aoi's life, they said nothing. Sato made them sign that they received the letter and turned to leave.

Aoi's heart filled. He could've fallen in love with Sato all over again. Still, the bill had to be outrageous, but it was worth every yen.

They walked out, and Aoi pulled at Sato's elbow.

"I can't believe you did that," Aoi said.

Sato held Aoi's hand. "We're better together, remember?"

Better words couldn't have been spoken. Aoi's stomach lurched, squeezing all the anxiety up to a trembling jaw. He closed his eyes. No other time would be more perfect. He reached into his pocket and hid the ring in his palm, but when he opened his eyes, Sato had already sunk to his knees, a small box in his hand.

"Aoi, I wrote out a whole speech on my way here, but right now all I can think of is how I want to be with you for the rest of my life. Please let me do it." Sato opened the box, a silver ring inside.

Aoi laughed and held out the ring he'd palmed. "You can't be proposing, because I was."

Sato stood and hugged Aoi in an embrace he never wanted release from. Sato's arms pulled them together, their chests pressed so close their heartbeats beat out their love in unison.

Aoi slipped his ring on Sato's finger. It was so big it slipped off. Sato chuckled and stuck it on his thumb. Sato took the same brushed silver ring and placed it on Aoi's, only getting as far as the first knuckle.

"I guess we need to exchange these for the right size," Sato said.

Aoi moved the ring to his pinkie, then laced their fingers together. Even if they were on the wrong fingers, the two matching rings couldn't look more perfect.

"Let's go home," Sato said.

They separated, and the line of women outside the restaurant clapped. Aoi's cheeks grew hot, but he didn't care that they saw.

EPILOGUE

Months later

SATO POPPED OPEN THE champagne bottle to a fizzy explosion of bubbles and laughter. He poured two glasses, and they crossed their arms to drink. There were more cheers and the flash of the photographer's camera.

After the cheers, Jin took over. Sato never thought he'd see the usual bondage gear and leather attire of the Lilith members be replaced with suits, but they stood before them dressed in perfect wedding attire. They'd played a soft-ballad remake of one of their songs, creating the perfect music for Aoi and Sato's wedding.

Aoi stepped down from the crate and strolled to their couple's table for dinner. Aoi's chair had a thick cushion resting on it.

"A cushion too?" Sato said.

"You saw how off balance the engagement photos were. There was that huge space between my head and yours."

Sato laughed. Aoi had insisted for all the non–full-body photographs of them together he'd use a crate so they could look almost at equal height.

"Have you decided where you want to go on the honeymoon yet?" Sato asked.

"I don't know. We'll have to wait until the second season of *Wild Skies* finishes recording."

"But after that. Any suggestions? We could go overseas."

"Flights can get so expensive overseas."

Sato laughed. Aoi almost didn't want to have a formal ceremony, but then the videos of them proposing at the same time popped up on the internet. Aoi's agent called a few days later, giving him a list of shops and venues donating items for when the happy day came.

"Okay, no overseas," Sato said. "So where in Japan?"

"Kyoto might be nice. They have all those festivals."

"Kyoto it is."

Aoi's hand slid underneath the tablecloth and rested on Sato's thigh. "I think I'm ready for dessert."

"We haven't even had dinner yet," Sato said.

Aoi leaned over and nibbled on Sato's ear. "I wasn't talking about food."

AUTHOR NOTE

THANK YOU SO MUCH for reading. When I first wrote the first *Would It Be Okay to Love You?* back in 2016, I thought by the time I got to the end, marriage equality would finally happen in Japan. Then they won the 2020 Olympic bid, and I thought for sure now it would happen since it would be embarrassing to hold such an event and still not have full equality for everyone. I was wrong. So *Year Three* is kind of my huge grumble with Japan. Of course it's not just Japan, but many other countries as well. I hope one day the whole word will unite to expand equal rights to everyone. I will keep fighting for it!

If you enjoyed *Year Three*, please leave a few words in a review. As an indie author, I don't have the same budget as the big publishers to spread the word of my books, so every review and mention of Aoi and Sato will help.

Thanks

Amy Tasukada

June 13, 2019

ABOUT THE AUTHOR

AS AN ONLY CHILD, Best Selling Author Amy Tasukada began putting her daydreams to paper at the young age of ten. She was inspired by Japanese literature, works from French classic authors like Marcel Proust, as well as tons and tons of yaoi/boys' love manga. However, there were only so many books that piqued her interest. Fueled by an obvious lack of books she wanted to read, Amy decided to write them herself.

Amy found her niche in the LGBT genre with Japanese influenced gay fiction. Though her works span a wide range — from gritty mafia thrillers to fluffy, contemporary romance, Amy uses her deadly, but delicate writing style to weave exciting tales of suspense, love, and gore, all under the supervision of her amazing editor (and calico cat), O'Hara.

While crafting her novels, Amy researches each setting extensively to paint the most colorful picture for her readers. She creates each story's setting in a way that has been described as "crisp and lyrical" by fans.

When she's not penning a new installment of her mafia series or attending a writing workshop, the North Texas author can be found drinking tea, reading, or filming J-fashion hauls on her YouTube channel.

CONNECT WITH AMY ON..

WWW.AMYTASUKADA.COM

FACEBOOK:
FACEBOOK.COM/AMYTASUKADAOFFICIAL/

YOUTUBE:
YOUTUBE.COM/USER/AMYTASUKADA

TWITTER:
TWITTER.COM/@AMYTASUKADA